CHASE A RAINBOW

When Sarah starts a new life as an hotelier in her father's homeland, she stirs up memories and family secrets. What is David, the local fisherman, afraid of — and why does his son Sebastian look familiar? Who is plotting against her? She falls in love with Jed, her mysterious handyman; but this can only bring pain, as he too is running away from another life . . . As pasts and present become entangled, can the heartaches finally be put to rest?

FAY WENTWORTH

CHASE A RAINBOW

Complete and Unabridged

LINFORD
Leicester

First published in Great Britain in 2006

First Linford Edition
published 2007

British Library CIP Data

Wentworth, Fay
    Chase a rainbow.—Large print ed.—
Linford romance library
    1. Love stories
    2. Large type books
    I. Title
    823.9'2 [F]

    ISBN 978–1–84617–798–9

Published by
F. A. Thorpe (Publishing)
Anstey, Leicestershire

Set by Words & Graphics Ltd.
Anstey, Leicestershire
Printed and bound in Great Britain by
T. J. International Ltd., Padstow, Cornwall

This book is printed on acid-free paper

1

'Are you really serious?' Davinia looked at her daughter in horror. 'Sarah, tell me you're joking. You haven't really bought this, this . . . ruin?'

'Rainbow's End,' Sarah murmured. 'I shall call it Rainbow's End.'

They were standing on a flagged path in front of the old stone building. The afternoon sun sparkled on the calm sea behind them and bounced rainbows across the mellow stones. The windows were grimy and the paintwork flaked, but the slated roof and twisting chimneys sat nobly against the stark mountain. Glowing heathers blazed across the rocks and birdsong echoed from the stunted trees.

'It's heavenly!' Sarah was gazing at the house with love in her eyes. 'Just imagine, Mum, with renovation and a lick of paint, this will be a retreat for

1

those who want a quiet holiday; walking, breathing fresh sea air . . . '

'Very fresh!' Davinia shivered and drew her thin jacket closer. 'It's at the back of beyond! Whoever would want to stay here?'

'Lots of people.' Sarah spoke determinedly. 'Not everyone likes the bright lights and hectic nightlife that you do, Mother. Some folk need to get away from all that, the stress of city life. Here they can relax. If the weather's right they can swim.' She gestured to the sea, lapping gently against the sea wall across the road. 'They can walk, climb.' She waved an arm at the mountain. 'And just listen to the silence!'

Davinia shuddered. 'Well, I think you're mad. Whatever would your father have said . . . '

'Dad would have loved it here!' Sarah's eyes filled with tears. 'He left that legacy for me to . . . '

'I know!' Her mother interrupted irritably. 'To chase your rainbow! What a silly thing to say in a will.' It still rankled. 'At least he made you wait until you were twenty-one. Perhaps he thought you might have gained some sense by then!'

'For heaven's sake, Mum, don't be so negative!' Sarah snapped. 'This is a business venture as well you know. I've always wanted a hotel, that's why I did that hotel management course, and I'm a fair cook, even though I do say so myself. What better than here, in Tremaine?

'The village is only a couple of miles away, and you can visit easily enough from London. Dad would have been proud that I wanted to return to his roots. He never enjoyed life in the city anyway.'

Davinia shrugged and turned away. She knew she was beaten. She still missed her calm, quiet husband more than she cared to admit.

All her friends at university had been amazed when she had married the studious accountant, Roger, and had predicted an early divorce. But, in their case, the old adage of 'opposites attract' had worked and they had been very happy.

Roger had adored his elegant blonde wife and had tempered Davinia's impetuosity, whilst she had tempted him from his cocoon of studies and shown him fun and laughter. His untimely death from a heart attack had rocked her safe world and she and Sarah had struggled to come to terms with his loss.

Now, three years on, Davinia still felt that loss in her heart; and Sarah longed for his forthright wisdom to help her follow her dream. She had been close to her father, inheriting his dark looks and quiet strength and they had talked frequently about her plans for the future.

'We might as well look inside.' Sarah stopped further discussion by opening the front door. 'Come on, Mum.'

The kitchen was large and airy with a view of the sea and the mountain. From the hall a large room stretched the front

4

of the house, bay windows boasting a vista that swept over the sea.

'The dining room,' Sarah breathed excitedly. 'And there's a downstairs washroom, larder, storerooms. Oh, Mum, it's perfect.'

'Eight bedrooms, all large,' Sarah was saying. 'Easy enough to convert to en-suite. And then there's the annexe, and behind that, an orchard. I'll put swings for the children and seats so that the guests can sit outside on balmy evenings . . . '

She was leaning through a window and Davinia peered down at the long stone building running at right angles to the house, directly beneath the mountain.

'I shall live in the annexe.'

'By yourself?'

'Of course, by myself!' Sarah laughed. 'Who do you think is sharing it with me?'

'Well, is it safe?' Davinia shivered. She had hope that Sarah would have settled with Alan, the son of her best friend, who was obviously head over heels in love with Sarah, but, so far, any arrangements on her part to encourage the friendship had met with a blank wall, and she was amazed to find that Sarah just wasn't interested in romance.

'I'll be fine, Mum, really.' Sarah spoke gently, aware of her mother's misgivings. She loved her mother dearly, but they lived on different wavelengths and she knew her mother would never understand; whereas her father . . . She squared her shoulders resolutely and led the way back downstairs.

'Let's go and find something to eat, Mum, and then you can race back to your safe city house!' Sarah spoke lightly. 'I've taken a room in the village for now, so I can organise the birth of Rainbow's End! The builders are calling round tomorrow.'

Tremaine boasted an attractive inn and restaurant and even Davinia had to concede that the meal was excellent. Slightly mollified, she settled into her

MG Roadster and, bidding Sarah a last farewell, she heaved a sigh of relief and set off for home.

Sarah let herself into her bedsit and sank onto the bed. At least her mother hadn't been awkward. Ever since she had bought the house she had worried about Davinia's reaction, their phone calls on the subject being terse and short. However, she was relieved that the initial inspection had gone better than expected.

Her thoughts flew briefly to Alan and his anger when he had learned of her plans. She had always been so careful not to encourage his advances. He was perfectly pleasant and no doubt would make somebody a steady and reliable husband, but settling into city life as a solicitor's wife, particularly when the solicitor in question did not share her dreams and was unfortunately lacking a sense of humour, was not part of her future plan!

Now she could concentrate on getting Rainbow's End shipshape in time for the spring, and hopefully, with advertising, her first visitors would arrive by summer.

Renovation seemed slow and, once the builders were organised, Sarah returned to London for Christmas. It took until May for Rainbow's End to show improvement. The annexe had been revamped first, making a cosy home for Sarah.

From her bedroom window she gazed across at the workmen bustling in and out of the back door and her living room window splayed on to the mountainside. Tumbling gorse reached almost to her wall and May blossom sprinkled the orchard hedges like a dusting of icing sugar.

Her own home at last, no more rented flats and polluting traffic. If she opened her window at night, she could hear the sound of the waves on the shingle, and the cry of the gulls on the rocks.

★　★　★

It was in response to her advert for a cook/housekeeper that Molly Palmer arrived on her doorstep. A lady of ample proportions, her grey curls bounced around her beaming face.

'Sarah, young Roger's daughter. Well, I never!' Molly's eyes were full of tears.

'You remember my father?' Sarah's heart was beating fast.

'Of course, dearie. A bright young thing, he was! We missed him when he went, we really did.' She shut her mouth suddenly. 'But that's another story.' Her voice became brisk. 'I gather you're wanting some help in the kitchen?'

'That's right. I'm opening Rainbow's End as a hotel. Simple holidays with good homemade cooking!'

Molly proved to be a real asset, coming in daily to help with the final preparations and producing young staff ready to wait on table. The next days were busy and Sarah had little time to think of her father, mentioning him only once.

'You must tell me all about my father, Molly.' They were indulging in a rare sit-down with a cup of coffee. 'There's so much I don't know about him and it's as if fate has intervened, with Rainbow's End coming up for sale, just like that.'

'It's certainly strange,' Molly agreed. 'Although properties round here are difficult to sell, especially old ones.'

'I'd love to see where my father was born.' Sarah's eyes misted. 'Will you take me there?'

Molly studied her thoughtfully for a moment and opened her mouth to speak. Hesitating, she suddenly clamped it shut and got up. 'There's work to do,' she announced and left the kitchen.

Sarah sat staring at the closed door. She felt uneasy, as if Molly were hiding something. Then she shrugged. Molly was right, there was work to do. But as soon as she could, she planned to explore Tremaine and find her father's birthplace.

Her mother phoned and wished her

luck as completion day arrived, but Davinia hadn't attempted another visit.

'I'll come in the summer.' Sarah could sense her mother's shiver down the phone. 'When it's warmer.'

By the beginning of June, the bookings were beginning to come in. She awoke each morning full of excitement and plans and the summer stretched expectantly before her.

She was happy with the staff she had so far, but her advert for an odd-job handyman had produced little response.

And then, one glorious June day when the sea bathed in the early sun that peeked from the mountain and the gorse raised golden blossoms from the dew, she looked up from her inspection of the dining tables and gazed at the front drive. There, parked across the whole access, was a caravan, a bright yellow caravan with blue daisies painted brashly over the sides!

'Talk about flower-power,' she muttered. 'I thought that went out in the sixties!'

11

She opened the front door and waited. From the battered car emerged a man. He seemed to unwind his large frame from the seat, towering above her in a rather formidable way. His broad shoulders stretched his red T-shirt to the limit of its seams and his dark waves tumbled chaotically to his shoulders.

He approached her purposefully, his brilliant eyes sweeping her small frame in one quick flash. She felt herself straighten her shoulders and stretch to her full height.

'Good morning.' His voice was surprisingly low and melodic. 'I understand you're looking for a handyman.'

She nodded, for a moment at a loss for words.

'Then I'm your man.' He grinned, showing perfect, even white teeth. 'I can undertake any job. I've my own tools and I'm strong.'

'I just need a corner to park Cynthia.' He waved towards the caravan. 'And I'm ready to start.'

Sarah pulled herself from her stupor.

She hadn't even interviewed the man yet and he was already giving orders! She frowned. He was very arrogant. She wasn't sure she wanted him to work for her at all and, as for Cynthia, where on earth was she to put a caravan? Besides, she realised, interviewing a prospective employee on the driveway was not to her advantage.

'Come into the office, Mr . . . ?'

'Jed, call me Jed, ma'am.' He bowed, but his eyes were mocking and she was uncomfortably aware of the frisson of tension that crept up her spine and tickled her heart.

2

'The name's Sarah.' She turned away. 'This way, er, Jed.' She led the way through the hall to her own apartment. She had neatly screened the corner of her living-room and turned it into an office. Jed settled himself rather uncomfortably on the small chair and, at last, she felt in control of the situation.

'Now, Jed,' she leaned across the table. 'Have you any references?'

'Of course.' He produced some rather crumpled sheets from his pocket and Sarah read the glowing statements. It appeared he could turn his hand to everything, and perfectly! Sarah wondered if they were forgeries.

'Well, Jed,' she cleared her throat. She certainly needed someone to help with the heavier work and this man seemed, on paper, to be just what she was looking for, but she hadn't anticipated taking on someone quite as uncomfortable as Jed, and, as for his caravan . . .

'Why did you leave your last job?' she enquired, feeling she must make some effort to conduct a reasonable interview.

'Hotel closed for the winter, I've been odd-jobbing around since last October. I was meandering along the coast, looking for work, and saw your job advertised in the shop in Tremaine. Seemed ideal for the summer, and here I am.'

He was lounging back in his chair, grinning at her and she had the distinct impression he was aware of her discomfort. He was a very attractive man, she acknowledged to herself, in his early thirties she guessed and then pulled herself back to the business in hand.

'Just for the summer?'

He shrugged. 'Maybe, maybe not, depends . . . '

'On what?'

'Whether I like it here.'

'And whether I like you,' Sarah thought, but she smiled. 'Well, Jed, shall we say a month's trial?'

They agreed terms and Sarah was surprised that he accepted her rather low wage.

'And Cynthia?' He stood up.

Her mind had been working on that. There was absolutely no way the caravan could be on show to the guests, but there was the orchard. She had plans for swings and seats, but the ground needed clearing and the fruit trees pruning first. If Jed cleared a corner by the wall, Cynthia would fit nicely out of sight.

She voiced her suggestion and he agreed with alacrity, following her to the back and surveying the land tucked into the lea of the mountain.

'Perfect,' he agreed.

'There's a track running up the side of the wall,' Sarah pointed out. 'And you can come in through that far gate. Perhaps you could clear some of the grass and brambles and make a comfortable site.'

'No problems,' he answered cheerfully. 'I'll soon settle in. Do you have a scythe?'

Sarah nodded. Her shed contained a large selection of gardening tools, very few used. 'Come with me.' She turned. 'If you can move Cynthia to the back . . . ' She frowned as he grinned and his eyes sparkled mockingly.

'Of course, ma'am.' He bowed again and Sarah felt irritation rise. 'I'll make Cynthia as inconspicuous as I can and then I'll have my tour of inspection before setting up camp. Alright if I start work tomorrow?'

He turned away before she could answer and, whistling, curled himself back into his car and started the engine.

Sarah breathed a sigh of relief as the caravan rounded the corner and she saw the roof disappear as he manoeuvred the track. Turning back into the hall she wondered if she had been foolish taking on a man like Jed, a man she knew nothing about, other than what was in his very doubtful references, and she didn't even know his surname.

Molly echoed her doubts when she came in to do some baking. 'We'll probably all be murdered in our beds!' she muttered after Sarah's rather lame explanation about Jed. 'Are you sure he's all right?'

Sarah nodded confidently. She couldn't have the staff upset and Molly was an absolute gem. 'He'll be fine,' she answered cheerfully. 'And we do need a man about the place, Molly. Wait until he's settled in and we'll soon get to know more about him.'

Molly grunted noncommittally and kneaded dough ferociously. 'When does Mr Ratton arrive?'

★　★　★

Sarah was nervously anticipating their first guest. 'He said he'd be here Saturday afternoon. In the meantime, Molly, I'll send Jed in here for a coffee,

18

you'll soon wheedle his life history out of him!'

Sarah laughed and returned to her office. She wished she felt comfortable about Jed, but if it didn't work out she could always ask him to leave. From her window she could see the roof of the caravan with its blue daisy emblazoned on its length and she couldn't suppress a smile. The man certainly had confidence if he could live in a van like that!

Sarah was pleasantly surprised when, a few hours later, she took him a jug of coffee. He had obviously worked hard all morning, clearing the grass, and the caravan was backed neatly against the stone wall, water containers and other paraphernalia stacked tidily in the corner.

For some reason Cynthia looked perfectly suited to its position and the orchard had taken on a new identity.

'You're all set up?' She held out the coffee.

'Thanks.' He took the pot from her

and placed it on a small table at the side of the van. 'Yes, this is brilliant! Such a perfect spot, I'm going to enjoy it here.'

'Good. You're welcome to make use of the staff bathroom, if you need to, and of course Molly will give you your meals when you're on duty.'

'Sounds great. Perhaps we could have a look around now, and discuss what you want me to do?'

'Of course.' Sarah waited while he finished his drink and then led him through Rainbow's End.

'What I need,' she explained, 'is someone who can do any maintenance or repair work, also to keep the front drive tidy, maybe do something about a garden, we've only pots at the moment. And then I'd like the orchard cleared, the gates painted, the back yard sorted . . . '

'So there's plenty to do then!' His voice held a hint of sarcasm, but when Sarah looked at him he was smiling.

'Yes, there is,' she answered shortly.

Why did she feel at such a disadvantage with this man? It was annoying. 'Come and meet Molly.' She led the way into the kitchen.

'Molly, meet Jed. Now, I have to go and make a couple of phone calls. Molly, can you give Jed a cup of tea and fill him in on the meals. I'll be back in a minute.'

She let out a big sigh as she closed the door on the kitchen and went to her rooms. Pouring herself a coffee she stared out of the window at the roof of Cynthia and let her tension ease. She smiled suddenly as she realised her mother was arriving at the weekend to stay for a couple of days.

* * *

Davinia stood on the driveway, her car door flung open, surveying the gaily-painted sign. 'Well,' her voice was grudging. 'I must say there's a vast improvement since I was last here. Well done, Sarah.'

She smiled at her daughter. 'I will admit I thought you'd taken on too much, but you've obviously got your father's determination and I can see you're succeeding.' She gave Sarah a hug. 'Now, if it's as nice inside, then I'll be really happy.'

As if on cue Jed appeared. 'Can I take your cases, ma'am?'

Davinia stared, for once bereft of words, as Jed came down the steps. Sarah hid a smile. He was certainly a hunk! His muscles bulged beneath his red T-shirt — he seemed to have a wardrobe full of red T-shirts. 'Thank you, Mr . . . ?' She smiled her provocative smile and Sarah sighed. 'Here we go again!' she thought.

'Just call him Jed, Mother,' Sarah spoke coolly. 'Thank you Jed, Room Six, if you don't mind.'

Jed winked and hefted the cases under his arms as if they were full of cotton wool. Davinia trotted on behind.

'When you've unpacked, I'll make you a coffee,' Sarah called after her and her mother waved a delicate hand over her shoulder.

'Where on earth did you find him?' Davinia settled herself into the chair in Sarah's front room and took the offered cup.

'He just appeared,' Sarah answered casually.

'Well!' Her mother looked at her suspiciously. 'I trust you know his background?'

'Of course!' Sarah hoped she sounded convincing.

Davinia look thoughtful. 'I gather he's not married. Doesn't seem to have any roots at all as far as I can tell.'

Sarah grimaced. Her mother had extracted more information from Jed in a few minutes than she and Molly had been able to glean in days.

'I know he's good looking and obviously extremely capable, but,' Davinia looked hard at her daughter. 'Are you sure he's . . . safe?'

'He seems perfectly 'safe' to me, Mother. He's very capable, strong and he doesn't mind what he does. At the moment, he's absolutely necessary to me.'

At that moment Molly burst through her door. 'Sorry, Sarah,' she was flustered, 'But it's the guest, Mr Ratton, he's arrived.' Sarah stood up.

'Jed will see him upstairs, Molly, Room Four.'

'You'll have to come, Sarah,' Molly was twisting her hands in her apron. 'He's not happy!'

Sarah sighed and, followed by Davinia, went into Reception. Peter Ratton was pacing the floor. A tall man, upright and spruce, he was bristling with indignation.

'Can I help you?' Sarah smiled her most winning smile.

'Are you the owner of this hotel?'

Sarah nodded. 'Well, I expected some sort of welcome,' he grunted. 'I came by train, took ages to get a taxi, and this place seems to be in the back of beyond. How do I get to civilisation?'

'Please, come and sit down.' Sarah

led the way into the lounge. 'Have a cup of tea.' She motioned to Molly who nodded and shot back to the kitchen. 'I'm sure you're tired after your journey.'

'Mr Ratton,' Davinia came forward holding out her hand, the very picture of civilisation. 'Do relax and tell me all about yourself. Do you know,' she sat elegantly opposite as Peter Ratton subsided into a chair. 'You're our very first guest, and we're honoured to receive you. I'm sure you'll find all you need for a totally enjoyable holiday, and, of course, transport can be arranged to Tremaine at any time.'

Sarah thought her mother was promising a bit much but, as her guest was almost smiling, she couldn't argue. By the time Molly arrived with a tray of tea and homemade cakes Mr Ratton appeared to be mollified and he and Davinia were chatting like old friends.

'Call me Peter, my dear.' He patted her hand. 'If I may call you Davinia?'

Her mother uttered that tinkling

laugh that floored most men and Sarah smiled. Perhaps she should employ her mother full time?

'He's a retired naval officer,' Davinia informed her later. 'Seems he's had rather a bad time lately. His wife died a few years ago and his son has just emigrated to Australia. Feeling lonely, you know? Anyway, he decided he needed a quiet holiday to relax and plan for his future, only his journey was awful and Rainbow's End seemed rather quieter than he anticipated.'

Sarah sighed. 'Honestly, Mother, I don't know how you do it!'

'I like people.' Davinia laughed. 'Besides, he's quite happy now, and looking forward to his stay.'

* * *

The next day Sarah waved her mother off with a guilty feeling of relief. At least Davinia seemed satisfied that her daughter was in control and she could now enjoy her hectic life without worry!

'Next time I'll bring Andrew. I'm sure he'd be impressed!' She didn't wait for her daughter's reply and Sarah groaned inwardly. The last thing she wanted was to entertain Andrew at Rainbow's End. Still, perhaps her mother would forget that particular promise, although Sarah had a niggling feeling she was not to be spared that visit!

Sighing she returned to the kitchen where Molly was preparing the evening meal. 'Jed wanted to see you,' Molly was energetically peeling vegetables. 'Something about having a night off?'

'Where is he?'

'Gone back to his van.' Molly had grudgingly agreed she could find nothing in Jed's manner that constituted a threat to their lives, but she had been unable to ferret out any information about his past, and that had made her rather aloof with him.

Sarah made her way into the orchard and found Jed sitting outside his caravan reading. She watched his face as she approached, his expression one of concentration and then suddenly, as if aware of her scrutiny, he raised his eyes and just for a moment their startling blueness drowned in hers and she felt suddenly vulnerable and very shy.

'Molly said you were looking for me.'

He waved to the chair opened on the grass. 'Your mother gone?' His grin was mischievous and she felt her awkwardness disappear.

''Fraid so.'

'Nice lady, your mother.' He spoke solemnly, but Sarah could see the twinkle in his eyes.

She sighed. 'She is. At least she's happy with Rainbow's End. She was totally against the idea originally.'

'I gather you take after your father?'

Sarah wondered just how much information Davinia had given Jed and studied him thoughtfully.

'He would have loved this,' she answered.

'So I gather.'

'You wanted to see me about time off?' She broke the quiet silence.

'If it's alright with you, I should like tonight off. If you've nothing lined up for me, of course.'

'That would be fine, Jed. We must agree on your free time, you're entitled to that.'

'I won't need much. Besides, I get breaks in between jobs. But tonight is important.'

'Then take it as read, Jed. Are you visiting someone special?' Sarah was annoyed at her curiosity, but surely it was normal to want some background on your employees?

Jed was watching her and shrugged. 'Just some business I have to deal with.'

Sarah suddenly felt anxious. 'You will stay for the season, won't you Jed?'

He smiled suddenly and leaned towards her. 'I have no intention of leaving,' his voice was soft. 'This set-up suits me ideally and, as long as we both agree, I shall stay until autumn.'

She had to be content with that.

Whatever was in his past, he obviously had no intention of divulging it. She stood up. 'Well, I'd better get back.' She spoke briskly; aware that he would know she was curious and suddenly annoyed with herself. What he did or had done was nothing to do with her.

He called in to her office just before he went. 'I've brought the keys to the shed, just in case you need anything.'

'Such as?' Sarah was eyeing his clothing in surprise.

'Well, a bulb may go or you may need tools for something!' He was laughing at her and she felt the flush rise in her cheeks.

'I'm sure we can manage for one night by ourselves!' Her voice was cool and she handed the keys back to him. 'I do keep a duplicate set of keys myself.'

'Fine, then I'll be off.' He pocketed the keys and walked swiftly from the room leaving her gazing pensively at the closed door.

For once he had removed the red T-shirt and was dressed in a smart grey suit and sparkling white shirt. She wondered what business it was that had commanded such an outfit.

She shook herself from her irritability and tried to concentrate on the book-keeping. It was none of her business; and, heaving a sigh, stared at the figures.

At last, her brain becoming dull with tiredness, she made herself a drink and decided to turn in for the night. Glancing out of the window she could see no reflection of light from the caravan. So Jed was still out. She looked at the clock. It was ten minutes to midnight.

She didn't hear Jed's car creep quietly into the orchard in the early hours. The alarm woke her with a start the next morning. Her first thought was of Jed and she was annoyed at her relief when she heard him whistling in the yard.

Later in the morning she took him coffee. She wanted to discuss the orchard and her ideas for improvement.

As she turned to leave, she couldn't stop herself asking, 'You had a good time last night?'

He studied her face, his own expression inscrutable. She felt her colour heighten. 'I had no problems.'

She thought this a strange reply, but refrained from further comment, feeling his sudden coldness wash over her.

'Come to the kitchen if you want more coffee.' She turned away, angry with herself and didn't see the rueful smile that crossed his face and softened his eyes.

Sighing, he surveyed the front of the hotel. Flowers to match the rainbow painted over the door, a rainbow bed either side of the drive. Already he was imagining the finished gardens and he reached into his pocket for a notebook. And the orchard, he could picture that too, his doodling expanded.

The afternoon stretched before her and Sarah decided to walk to the village. She wandered down the main street and studied the windows of the various bric-a-brac tourist shops that gaily scattered the pavements with buckets and spades and all the necessities of seaside holidays.

She stopped outside the bow windows of the artists' shop. The window display showed watercolours, mainly scenes of the harbour and views from the beach. They were beautifully done and the sort of holiday mementoes tourists would buy but, peering through the glass, she could see other pictures festooning the walls.

Pushing open the door she wandered in. A bell sounded in the dim recesses and then a man appeared. Tall and blond, his piercing eyes, eyes the colour of the deep sea in the sunshine, swept over her.

'Sarah Morgan,' he said quietly.

Sarah was startled. 'And you are?'

He hesitated. 'Sebastian.' He held out his hand and grinned, the smile lightening his features. 'The local artist. I heard you had bought Rainbow's End.'

'The village gossip?' Sarah laughed. 'I expect Molly had informed everyone of my existence!'

'Too true,' he agreed. 'I'm glad you've finally got around to visiting the locals.'

'It's been a busy time,' Sarah was immediately defensive.

'Of course,' he answered smoothly, his eyes assessing and Sarah was suddenly hit by a memory. A faint, shadowy memory that stirred on the edge of her mind but refused to take shape. She had seen Sebastian before.

'Do I know you?'

'I doubt it.' His voice was cool and she felt his withdrawal.

The bell sounded again and a customer entered the shop. Bidding Sebastian a hasty goodbye Sarah left and wandered slowly towards the harbour.

She was sure Sebastian was familiar, and, as she watched the small boats bobbing on the incoming tide, she felt that feeling of unease that she had experienced with Molly. Tremaine was her father's home, and held secrets, and she wondered again if she should have disturbed the past.

3

The following morning Sarah was sitting at the kitchen table checking her guest list while Molly baked.

'We've a family coming at the end of July, with a young child, so we'll give them the one family room. Then there's a couple from London wanting a brochure. Guests might be sparse at the moment, Molly, but at least they're starting to book.'

'We had that nice young couple on honeymoon last week.' Molly smiled as she remembered the lovey-dovey pair.

'And they stayed an extra two days, so they must have liked it here!'

'They enjoyed the peace and quiet I think. There were those two hikers as well.'

'Oh, yes,' Sarah said. 'It's all coming along nicely.' She laughed. 'And we've still got Peter Ratton. I thought he'd be the first to leave!'

There was a knock on the kitchen door. 'Come in,' Sarah looked up as the object of their last comment poked his head around the door. 'Talk of the devil . . . '

Peter Ratton raised his eyebrows.

'Sorry.' Sarah blushed. 'What can I do for you Mr Ratton?'

'Can I have a word?'

Sarah wondered what was wrong this time, but she saw that he was smiling. 'Come into the lounge.' She picked up her paperwork. 'Could we have coffee, Molly?'

'Of course.' Molly dried her hands. 'I'll bring it through.'

'Now,' Sarah held out a cup, 'What can I do for you, Mr Ratton?'

'Please, call me Peter.' He smiled and settled back in his chair. 'May I say first of all what a marvellous hotel you are running.'

Sarah was delighted, and surprised. 'I'm glad you approve.' She waited.

'The thing is, my dear,' Peter Ratton hesitated and took a sip of his coffee. 'I had rather a bad time before I arrived, so I'm afraid I was in a foul temper on my first day.'

Sarah thought it prudent not to comment.

'But I've really settled in now and I'm enjoying the peace and quiet. Of course, your mother ... such a delightful lady. Will she be returning soon?'

Sarah suppressed a smile. 'I'm sure she'll be making a visit before long, Peter.'

'I do hope so.' Peter appeared to be lost in thought. 'However,' he pulled himself back to the present, 'the reason I asked to see you, I was wondering if it would be inconvenient if I stayed for longer?'

'Of course not, I'd be delighted!' Sarah was thrilled. 'As you will have noticed, we're not exactly fully-booked as yet. But this is the first summer of opening so it will take time to build up a reputation. How long had you got in mind?'

'Well, most of the summer, I think. I'm interested in nature you know, always have been, and the birds and wild flowers round here are magnificent. I had thought I might produce a booklet on the subject.'

'I'm sure that would be very useful,' Sarah murmured. 'And something we could put on display for our guests.'

Peter Ratton looked gratified and finished his coffee. 'Thank you, my dear. Now that's settled I can relax and get on with my notes. If there's anything I can do to help at any time, please don't hesitate to ask.' He leaned forward and patted Sarah's hand. 'I think you're a very brave girl and I wish you every success with your project.'

Sarah smiled and rose. 'Thank you, Peter. I'll look forward to seeing your booklet.'

She returned to the kitchen and gave Molly the good news. Molly was looking rather flustered.

'The dough's not rising,' she announced irritably. 'And there's still the vegetables to do!'

'I think you need an assistant in the kitchen,' Sarah said. 'I'll put an advert with Mrs Williams in Tremaine Stores and see if we can get you some help in the mornings. A girl could do the preparation for you and leave you to get on with the cooking.'

Molly looked at her gratefully. 'I would appreciate it, Sarah. I didn't like to ask, seeing as how we're not so busy, but when there's guests it does get a bit hectic.'

'Don't worry. We'll sort something out before the next visitors arrive. The Stores have always come up trumps before, so we'll try them first.'

⋆ ⋆ ⋆

She was making her way across the yard when Jed came towards her. 'Good morning, Jed.'

'Ah, Sarah.' He towered in front of

her. 'I was wondering if it was all right if I went to fetch my boat?'

'Boat?'

'Yes, I've got a small fishing boat. It's moored up the coast, not far, but I see you've got moorings here and I'd like to bring her down if I may. We could do a spot of fishing — fresh fish for dinner?' He smiled.

'That sounds wonderful!' Sarah smiled. Jed never ceased to surprise her.

'Only it means I have to catch a bus and then sail back, so it could take most of the day.'

'No need for that, Jed. I've got to go into Tremaine so I can easily drive you a few miles farther on.'

'Are you sure?' He looked pleased and Sarah felt her heart lift. A morning out with Jed sounded enticing and perhaps she might glean some information about him!

'Oh, and Jed, there's a family coming at the end of the month. They've got a small boy. I was wondering if there was any chance we could fix a swing up by then?'

'I've been thinking about that.' Jed's voice was full of enthusiasm.

'Come into the office.' Sarah led the way. 'You've got some ideas?'

'Indeed, yes.' Jed leaned forward in his chair. 'In fact, we could kill two birds with one stone. Where I worked before, there was a warehouse. We could call there if you like. They produce excellent picnic tables and also, I was thinking, one of these large wood and rope climbing frames for the children.'

A grin spread across Sarah's face. 'Jed, that sounds wonderful.'

Leaving Molly in charge, she backed her car out of the garage and waited for Jed to curl his red T-shirted frame into her front seat. They set out in high spirits.

The warehouse proved to be as good as Jed had promised. Ordering six picnic tables for delivery she left the choice of climbing frame and ropes to Jed. Eventually, having signed a rather large cheque, they returned to the car feeling satisfied with the purchases.

'Oh, Jed, Rainbow's End is really taking shape at last,' she breathed. 'It's going to be everything I hoped for.'

He smiled at her enthusiasm. 'Of course it is, Sarah.' His voice was soft, 'I could see your vision in your first orders to me!'

She blushed. 'It is exciting, isn't it, Jed?' she echoed. 'Dad would have been so proud.'

'I'm sure he would.'

'Where are your parents, Jed?'

'Abroad.' His voice had turned cool. 'Father works for the Embassy in Africa. They've spent most of their married life abroad, so I haven't seen much of them really.'

'How sad. You didn't travel with them?'

'A little, during the holidays. But I went to school in this country.'

'You must have missed them.'

He shrugged. 'I was brought up like that, so I didn't really know anything

43

different. I had a good schooling and tremendous holidays!' He grinned.

'And what have you done with that good schooling?' she teased, for once completely relaxed in his company. She was enjoying the day out. 'Bought a boat to fish and a caravan?'

He chuckled. 'I didn't waste it. I did a business course and studied financial matters. I even became a financial adviser for a while.' He was staring out of the window.'

'Really?'

'I got fed up of the rat race and bought Cynthia.' His tone became abrupt and his face now held the shuttered look that she knew so well. Sarah sighed. His confidences had come to an end. But at least she knew something about his background now.

'A financial adviser?' She tried to lighten the mood again. 'At least now I know where to come to when I get into financial difficulties!' She laughed and a grin dispelled his grim expression.

'My fees are high,' he joked.

The talk turned to mundane topics and soon they were alighting at a small harbour.

She followed Jed to a boat that bobbed on the waves. Gaily painted white and blue — at least there were no daisies, Sarah thought — the small cabin gave refuge from the winds and the deck was piled with baskets and rope, a narrow wooden bench skirting the outside.

Sarah was suddenly swamped with memories of her childhood holidays, fishing with her father in a hired boat, his love of the sea taking her out for days, teaching her all the tricks he had learned as a child, and her eyes misted over.

'It's a lovely boat, Jed.' Her voice was husky. 'I should love to go out in her sometime.'

He looked at her in surprise. 'Of course you can, Sarah. I'd be delighted to take you out.'

'Please.' She smiled at him.

The boat turned on the tide and she

read the name 'Cynthia' on the side. 'Another Cynthia?' She laughed.

'I've always loved the name,' he grinned, 'and I couldn't think of a different one that was suitable. So I settled for Cynthia and Cynthia!'

* * *

On the journey home she thought about the complex man that was her handyman. A financial adviser building swings in her orchard. She wondered what had really decided him to leave a good career and found her thoughts drifting over his background.

Had there been a woman involved? Was that why he was so difficult to get to know? She sighed.

She had enjoyed the morning and his company more than she cared to admit. She mustn't let him get under her skin.

On the way back to Rainbow's End she called at Tremaine Stores and placed an advert with Mrs Williams for kitchen help.

'I'm sure there'll be a lass in the village wanting summer work, Sarah,' Annie Williams said. 'They're all wanting pocket money. I'll see who applies and give you a ring.'

'That would be fine, Mrs Williams. Thanks. You know the youngsters better than I so perhaps you could recommend one or two?'

'That'll be no problem.'

As Sarah emerged from the Stores, Sebastian was locking up the front door of his art gallery. He stared at Sarah as she crossed to her car. Feeling his gaze she swung round, her brow furrowing as she stared at him.

Where on earth had she seen him before? He gave her a brief salute and set off down the path to the harbour. Shaking her head she drove home, her thoughts worrying.

She would have been even more worried if she could have heard the conversation between Sebastian and his parents, Susan and David, as they sat at the table in Stoney Cottage that was crafted into the rock at the edge of the harbour.

'I think you ought to visit Sarah, Mum.' Sebastian was slicing bread. 'I'm sure she recognises me.'

Susan gave a sigh and glanced sideways at her husband's frowning face. 'I know,' she said. 'It's just so difficult.'

'I don't want to meet the girl,' David interrupted, his voice angry.

'Now, now, dear, don't get yourself upset. You know what the doctor said.'

'Blow the doctor! Just because I've had a slight heart attack, doesn't mean I can't think anymore!' He stomped out of the room and slammed the door.

'Oh dear.' Susan sank into a chair. 'What shall I do, Sebastian?'

'Don't worry, Mum.' Sebastian put his arms round his mother and she leaned against him gratefully. 'You look after Dad. I'll deal with this, somehow. As Sarah's obviously staying, she's got to know. Leave it to me.'

He sighed as he buttered his bread.

Why in heaven's name did Sarah have to turn up in Tremaine? Life was difficult enough without any further complications. It would have to be sorted out, and soon. Perhaps he could persuade his mother to visit Sarah without telling his father?

Tremaine was too small a village for gossip not to reach Sarah's ears. He was surprised that Molly hadn't let the cat out of the bag by now. But then, Molly was loyal and she wouldn't want to upset Sarah or Susan.

He gazed morosely out of the window and watched as a small fishing boat rocked gently through the harbour. 'Cynthia,' he murmured. That wasn't one of the regulars. He watched as it sailed right on through and headed towards the point.

'Rainbow's End,' he muttered to himself. 'That's where it's heading. Must be that new handyman she's taken on. I heard he'd got a boat. As long as he doesn't take all Dad's fish!'

Fish stocks were low on the coast

now and his father's fishing boat didn't bring in half the catch it used to. One of the stresses that had attributed to his heart attack, Sebastian thought now and the last thing his Dad needed right now was more stress! And the S for Sarah stood for S for Stress; as sure as fish was fish!

The boat slowly rounded the point and Sebastian wondered who the second crew member was.

The next morning, Sarah wandered down to the sea wall, taking deep breaths of the early tide and saw Cynthia moored on the jetty in the lea of the cliff, safe from the rocks.

The boat slapped against the waves and tugged at her rope as if aware that the tide was in and early morning was the time to fish.

On an impulse Sarah headed up the lane to the orchard. She had a longing to be out on the sea and now, while the hotel was quiet, was an opportunity to do just that. She would arrange to go fishing.

The caravan seemed quiet; there was no sign of Jed, so she knocked gently on the door. Perhaps he was already up and about his duties, although she hadn't seen a sign of him anywhere.

There was a scuffle from inside and then the door opened. The smile froze on her face as she stared at the apparition there. A young and tousled blonde, a red T-shirt billowing over her legs, rubbed her eyes and stared right back.

'Who are you?' Sarah's voice sounded hoarse to her own ears.

'Hello, I'm Lucy. Who are you?'

4

'Can I take a message?' Lucy's voice floated after Sarah as she beat a hasty retreat. The sight of the girl in the red T-shirt had left her speechless, and angry.

She marched down the lane and headed for the beach. She needed the fresh wind from the sea to clear her mind.

She kicked off her shoes and stomped across the sand. The waves crashed on the shore, foam spraying her lightly and the smell of the beached seaweed assayed her nostrils. She took a deep breath.

After all, she thought, as she bent to pick up an unusual shell, it was none of her business. Who Jed had in his caravan was nothing to do with her, but the girl had looked so young and Sarah was sure she could never see Jed in one of his T-shirts again without being reminded of the scene she had just witnessed.

She could see the sea — Cynthia bobbing on the waves. It looked lovely and she was reminded again of the holidays farther down the coast at Aberystwyth with her father.

She could hear his voice as they stood on the deck of the hired boat several miles out to sea. 'Hold the rod steady, Sarah. Dip gently, wind up and, there, you have one!' And she would reel in the thrashing mackerel, thrilled that she had caught supper. Davinia had stayed on the beach, sunning herself, and father and daughter deepened their bond on their expeditions.

She slipped her sandy feet into her sandals and traipsed back to the hotel. Standing for a moment in the driveway she surveyed her dream. It certainly looked bright and welcoming.

★   ★   ★

The rainbow sign glinted in the early sun and the gardens either side of the drive had been planted with geraniums, petunias and golden marigolds. They looked lovely. Jed certainly knew his gardening, whatever his personal faults. Wryly, she entered the kitchen.

'Morning, Molly.'

Molly glanced at her shrewdly. 'Been for a walk?'

Sarah nodded. 'I needed a breath of fresh air.'

'Jed's been in. Said you were looking for him?'

'I'll see him later,' Sarah answered casually. 'It wasn't important.

'Said he had to go into Tremaine, on business. He'll be back by twelve.'

'That's fine.' Sarah glanced out of the window as she heard Jed's car in the lane. Over the wall she could just make out two heads, one with short blonde hair. Some business! she thought, and hoped the business was now dressed in decent clothes.

She started checking the shelves. 'I

need to go into Tremaine myself.' She jotted notes on her list. 'I'll call at the cash and carry and replenish stocks. Anything we need, Molly?'

The older woman shook her head. 'Some help?' she asked hopefully.

'I've put an advert in the Stores. I'll call and ask Mrs Williams if there's been any response. If not, I'll try the local press. Molly,' Sarah hesitated, 'I went into the art shop the other day and met Sebastian. Do you know him?'

She saw Molly's hand still for a moment as she peeled potatoes. 'Oh, yes, I know Sebastian. Lived here all his life.'

She stared out of the window for a moment. 'He lives with his parents, Susan and David, in Stoney Cottage. That pretty stone cottage that looks as if it's built into the rocks down on the quay. David's a fisherman. Can't do too much now, though, since he had a heart attack.'

Molly banged the saucepan lid and reached for some vegetables. 'You've never been to Tremaine before?' she asked Sarah suddenly.

Sarah shook her head.

'Why did you come now?'

'My father was born here, so I understand. I wanted to see his birthplace and Rainbow's End was up for sale. It seemed like fate somehow.'

'Did he never talk about his home?'

Sarah shook her head again. 'We went to Aberystwyth for all our holidays, he loved it there. He said he'd been born on the coast, farther up, but never mentioned a village or town by name.

'I asked him several times, but he was very vague and we thought maybe his home had been a cottage in the country that was no longer there. He loved the sea, but his business kept him in town.'

'And your mum?'

'She was born in London. She put up with the holidays. I think she quite enjoyed the peace for a short while, but she's a city person.' Sarah smiled. 'She and Dad were so happy, really; like chalk and cheese, but they loved one another.'

'Good.' Molly's voice was gruff.

'We didn't find out Tremaine was actually his birthplace until after his death, and then curiosity got the better of me, and the rest is history as they say.' Sarah laughed.

'Anyway, Molly, enough gossiping. I must go and change the beds. The laundry van will be here and nothing's ready!'

It was after lunch before Sarah saw Jed again.

This time he was alone and she had regained her equilibrium.

'You were looking for me, Sarah?' His eyes were quizzical as he watched her and she saw a smile quirk his lips.

'Oh, yes, Jed.' Her voice was deliberately casual and she stared directly into the dark eyes. 'It wasn't important. I saw your boat moored and fancied a trip, but any time will do.'

'How about tomorrow morning?' he suggested, a twinkle in his eye. 'We could catch the early tide and reel in some mackerel. I've spare rods, I'll teach you to fish.'

'That sounds great, Jed.' Her voice was cool. Teach her to fish indeed! She could probably teach him a thing or two. Anyway, she wasn't going to enlighten him. But an early morning sail tempted her.

Turning away as nonchalantly as she could, she studied the notebook in her hand and didn't move her head as he walked away. Letting out a deep sigh, she went and checked the unoccupied rooms.

* * *

The next morning dawned bright and clear. Sarah could hear the waves lapping on the shore, the high wind of the day before seemed to have abated and as she leaned out of her window it seemed to be the perfect morning for a boat trip.

She had told Molly of her intentions

and other than a knowing glance, Molly hadn't commented.

Now Sarah dressed hastily and pushing a cardigan into her rucksack, she went downstairs. She had already cut sandwiches and she added some apples and a bottle of water. Jed obviously had had similar thoughts because he also sported a bulging rucksack.

'I always get hungry on the sea.' Sarah grinned.

'Me, too,' Jed replied. 'Shall we go?'

Sarah's heart was light as they made their way down to the rocks. Whatever Jed's private life, nothing was going to spoil her morning out on the boat. It had been so long since she had sailed, and come what may, she was going to enjoy it.

She had promised she would be back to help prepare the lunch but several hours stretched ahead of her and she sighed contentedly.

The water was icy on her ankles as she walked to the boat. Pulling herself on board, she stashed her bag in the cabin and waited for Jed to pull up the anchor. They drifted slowly out on the waves, Jed oaring the boat until it was clear of the rocks.

Then the motor purred into life and Cynthia shot forward, the sudden thrust upsetting Sarah's balance. Clutching the side of the boat, she took a deep breath as the wind whipped her hair.

She felt a surge of familiar exhilaration as the shore receded and the gulls wheeled overhead. Oh, she had left it too long!

'There are seals in the bay,' Jed called above the roar of the engine. 'Haven't seen them for a while, but they're around somewhere.'

'Wonderful.' Sarah searched the heaving water but there was no sign of the shining dark bodies. 'Perhaps they'll surface later.'

'Perhaps.' Jed laughed at her enthusiasm. 'This is great. I haven't been out fishing for weeks.'

'Amazing,' Sarah agreed and settled on the wooden seat, holding tightly to the side of the boat. The water was slightly choppy but nothing untoward and Sarah relaxed, allowing her mind to dwell only on the waves and the seabirds and Rainbow's End, now a doll's house in the distance.

Jed cut the engine. He had been watching his scanner. 'There's mackerel about,' he said. 'I think we'll give it a go.'

Sarah roused herself from her reverie and watched as Jed brought two fishing rods from the cabin. Hers was a neat one, smaller, but sturdy and she smiled as Jed threaded the line and attached hooks. If he wanted to wait on her, she wasn't going to discourage him.

His face was set in concentration and she watched as his deft hands avoided the barbed hooks. Long fingers, brown from the outdoor life he led, and his body was lean and taut. Sarah couldn't help noticing his muscles as his shirt — red again

— stretched over the top of his arms.

She sighed. He was a very attractive man, and dangerous if she allowed him to be. He had already assaulted her emotions more than she cared to admit. Somehow, she had to get a grip on herself. She conjured up a picture of Lucy and immediately felt her heart steady.

'There we are.' Jed stood in front of her. 'Now, drop the line overboard.'

She turned away from him, holding the rod in both hands. She felt his body heat against her back and steeled herself.

Leaning round her, his hands held her rod and she felt the bareness of his arms against her flesh. She groaned inwardly and watched the swinging hooks, silver flyers glinting in the sunshine.

'Unlock the reel and let the line drop into the water. Slowly, or you'll have a crow's nest if the line drops too quickly. It's a devil to unravel. The weight will take it to the bottom. There we go.'

Sarah let him guide the line through her fingers and, when he was satisfied the weight had reached the bottom, he moved away. Sarah felt a sudden coldness in her bones.

Sarah leaned against the side of the boat tugging gently on its anchor and her thoughts drifted back to Aberystwyth. She felt the line sway with the movement of the depths and let out a sigh of satisfaction.

This was so good. Without thinking she started to reel in, slowly, dipping her line up and down as she did so, just as her father had taught her. Suddenly she felt a bite. Whipping the line up, she knew she had hooked her prey. Laughing excitedly she turned and found Jed watching her, an angry expression on his face.

'I've caught one!' She'd forgotten the adrenalin rush and, too late, she realised that Jed was glaring at her accusingly.

'You've fished before!'

'Of course, my father taught me.' She

started to giggle as the fish jerked her line backwards and forwards. Reeling in, she felt the weight.

'So you thought you'd make a fool of me.' Jed was standing, arms akimbo, on the swaying deck.

'Oh, Jed. It wasn't that.' Sarah was wrestling with her line. This was no mackerel! She was having difficulty keeping upright. 'Please, Jed, I'm sorry. You were so sure of yourself — you could have asked.'

She realised her mistake. In her anger she had offended Jed's ego and, for a man like Jed, that was unforgivable. Blast the man.

'Jed, please,' she begged. Whatever she had got on her line was putting up the battle of the waters. 'I think I've hooked a whale! I can't hold the rod.'

She was struggling to hang on as the rod bent almost double under the thrashing water. She stopped reeling in. 'Please, Jed!' She was panicking now and knew she'd have to let go if she didn't have help.

'You're the expert, reel it in yourself!' He turned his back on her and started to pull up the anchor.

Sarah was speechless. The stupidity of the man! Couldn't he see she was in serious difficulties? Gritting her teeth, she wedged her feet against the side of the boat and leaned back.

All she could hope for was that the line would break. She would lose the weight and feathers, but that hardly mattered, but she mustn't let go of the rod!

Suddenly the water went calm and her line slackened. Breathing a sigh of relief, she relaxed. Too late she realised her mistake. A sudden terrific jerk on the line sent Sarah sprawling against the edge of the boat.

Gripping the rod in grim determination, the last thing she heard before she plummeted into the sea was Jed's shout.

The water closed over her head and bubbles echoed in her ears. Losing the rod, she clawed her way to the surface.

Gasping for breath and choking, she saw the lifebelt.

Clutching it with both arms, she was dragged unceremoniously over the edge of the boat, landing in a sodden heap at Jed's feet.

'You silly fool!'

'You stupid man, you!' Sarah retaliated and promptly burst into tears.

Jed was quick to fetch a blanket and, helping her to her feet, he wrapped her in it and held her against him.

'You frightened me!' His breath was warm on her wet hair and she clung miserably to the blanket. 'You could have hit your head and drowned.'

She looked up at him, shivering beneath the blanket. His eyes had deepened with concern and suddenly, as her eyes met his, they were both silent. For a moment they stood immobile, their bodies locked together and then he bent his head and his lips found hers, salty from the sea.

She felt the warmth flow through her and closed her eyes. Her stomach wrenched and nothing mattered. She forgot about being wet and cold, she forgot her anger, and gave herself totally to the bliss of his kiss.

Even Lucy was swept from her mind in the blind passion that raged through her. Releasing her slowly, he felt her shiver.

'Let's get you dry,' he said brusquely, a quiver in his voice, and she felt suddenly ice cold as he released her.

'I lost the rod,' she wailed, tears of frustration coursing down her cheeks.

'My fault.' His voice was calm again and he rubbed her down. 'Let's get you a hot drink and then we can continue the recriminations!'

He poured coffee from a flask and she sipped gratefully as the boat rocked gently in the swell. The sun was already drying her clothes and she had stopped shivering.

'Now.' He kneeled in front of her. 'I think we'd better get you home, and leave fishing until another day.'

'I'm sorry!' she muttered.

'So am I,' he answered gently and rubbed weed from her arm. 'No harm done. I've other rods.'

Sarah felt the tears well up again. Falling into the sea had shocked her and it hadn't been until she had sunk in the depths that she realised they hadn't been wearing lifejackets. Fishermen didn't, she knew that, but, all the same, they had been very foolish.

Jed wiped the tears from her cheeks and suddenly wrapped his arms around her in a bear-like hug. She smelled the salt on his body as her face pressed against his chest and she almost choked on her tears. She felt so safe in his arms.

He didn't kiss her again, much as she longed for him to do so, but their closeness was exquisite and she was almost grateful for her unexpected plunge.

A sudden vision floated into Sarah's head and she pulled away. 'Who's Lucy?' she gulped before she could stop herself, her emotions completely exposed.

Jed laughed. 'Is that what all this was about?' He was teasing her again and she wiped her tears with the back of her hand. 'You goose, Lucy is my sister!'

'Your sister?'

Jed nodded and moved away. 'With the parents away, I'm the only family she's got. But she's inclined to get herself into scrapes.' He sighed. 'That's why she's here in Tremaine. On the run, so to speak.'

Sarah was still grappling with the knowledge that Lucy was his sister and she felt a great weight lift from her heart. So the scene in the caravan wasn't what she had imagined at all! Lucy was his sister. She felt her cheeks burn. What a fool she was.

She turned. Jed was watching her, a smile on his face and she felt her blush deepen. 'Don't worry, she won't be a nuisance. I've put her in lodgings with Mrs Williams in Tremaine. She'll be fine there until I can sort her out.'

Sarah had no reply and watched as Jed pulled in the anchor and started

Cynthia for home. What had promised to be a fishing morning had turned into something completely different and she was torn between joy and regret. She sighed, feeling her hair drying stickily on her scalp. What a mess she must look!

★   ★   ★

Rainbow's End grew larger as they silently motored home. As they approached the jetty, Sarah saw figures on the beach. That was not what she needed, a welcome party that would see her in this sorry state! Perhaps they were walking and would move away.

There was no such luck. Jed pulled the boat expertly against the moorings and jumping into the waves, secured Cynthia with ropes. Sarah splashed morosely to the shore.

'Sarah, what on earth's happened?' Her mother's shrill voice deepened her confusion. Why on earth hadn't Davinia let her know she was coming?

'Good grief, Sarah, are you all right?'

Sarah raised her head in horror. There, standing next to her mother, looking immaculate in his dark grey suit, was Alan. He put a solicitous arm around her damp shoulders and surveyed Jed coldly.

'Would you mind telling me what you have done to my fiancée?'

5

'Well?' Alan stood, his arms tightening around her shoulders. 'What's been going on, Sarah. And who's this?'

Sarah pushed Alan away. 'For heaven's sake, I need a shower!'

Davinia caught Alan's arm. 'I'm sure there's a perfectly reasonable explanation.' She flashed Jed a winsome smile. 'Isn't there?'

Jed had turned away at Alan's words and was securing the boat. Ignoring both Davinia and Alan he set off up the path behind Sarah, his expression thunderous.

Sarah stormed into Rainbow's End, ignoring a startled Molly and went to her room. Running the shower full on, she stood under the hot flow and let the tension ease from her body. What a disaster. Slowly her equilibrium returned and a smile twitched at the corner of her mouth. What a sight she must have looked!

Then she remembered Alan's words, 'What have you done to my fiancée?' and she frowned. What on earth had possessed Alan? She had been quite explicit at their last meeting. She was not interested in a romance with him. Couldn't he take plain speaking?

Dressing herself hurriedly she was brushing her hair when there was a knock at her door. It was her mother.

'Can I come in?' Davinia's expression was anxious and she closed the door quietly as Sarah beckoned her in.

'Why on earth didn't you let me know you were coming?' Sarah's voice was irritable. 'I wouldn't have gone out in the first place. And what is Alan doing here?'

She turned to face her mother as Molly pushed the door open with some steaming coffee. 'Thanks, Molly,' Sarah took a mug gratefully, 'I need that.'

Davinia sat opposite her, fidgeting with her handbag. 'I wanted to come and see how you were getting on.' Her voice was plaintive. 'Alan is thinking of booking Rainbow's End for a conference, so I thought it would be an ideal opportunity for him to look the place over.'

Sarah sighed. 'A telephone call would have helped,' she said gently. 'At least I'd have been prepared.' She thought for a moment. 'What conference?'

Davinia brightened. 'Some sort of solicitors' conference. They have one every year, to, er, discuss things. Apparently it's Alan's turn to organise it and he thought he'd do you a favour and book Rainbow's End this year. He really is awfully fond of you.'

'I know,' Sarah answered dryly. 'But that's no excuse to call me his fiancée.'

'I think he was just worried, dear. Molly said you'd gone out on the boat with Jed, and the sea looked terribly rough. And then, when you came back you were all wet and bedraggled . . . He was concerned.'

'He has no need to be. I was perfectly

safe with Jed. I fell in, that's all. Jed pulled me out and we came back. No problems.'

'No?' Her mother's eyes narrowed. 'Should you have been out with Jed in the first place?'

'We were only fishing, mother, for goodness sake! Hardly a dangerous pursuit.'

'Hmm.' Davinia compressed her lips. 'I hope Jed is behaving himself.'

'Behaving himself? Really, mother!' Sarah said in exasperation. 'Of course, he's 'behaving himself'.'

'Anyway,' Sarah got to her feet, 'you go and settle in your room. At least we've got empty beds at the moment, and I'll get Molly to make up one of the single rooms for Alan. That reminds me,' she grimaced, 'I need to speak to Alan.' She marched out, her mother following.

'Don't forget he wants to make a big booking,' Davinia called after her as she disappeared down the hall.

'Ah well . . . ' Davinia sighed. How

she would like to see Sarah settled. And Alan was so suitable. Now, where was that lovely Jed to carry her cases up the stairs? She set off for the kitchen.

Alan was standing in the lounge surveying the heaving ocean through the bay window. The sun dappled the driveway and even in her anxiety, Sarah felt a thrill at the view. Alan turned as he heard the door close.

'Ah, Sarah, I need to talk to you.' He had on his most pompous expression and looked at Sarah as if she were a naughty child.

'No, Alan,' Sarah forestalled him, 'Sit down, I need to talk to you.'

Slightly uncertainly Alan sat in one of the leather chairs. Sarah sat opposite, balanced on the edge of the seat, her hands tightly clasped.

'Alan, this has to stop.'

'What's that?' His eyes widened.

'I am not your fiancée and, I'm sorry, but I never will be.' She tried to keep the anger out of her voice.

'Oh that.' He studied her for a

moment. 'I'm sorry, Sarah. I've been thinking about you such a lot. I've missed you so badly. The word just slipped out.' He shrugged and smiled. 'I was so worried about you. Out on the sea, with that chap. And then, when I saw you in such a state I couldn't contain myself. You need taking care of, Sarah.' He leaned forward persuasively. 'I want to take care of you.'

Sarah sighed. 'Alan . . . ' How on earth could she get through to him? 'Alan, I do not need taking care of! I am quite happy. Rainbow's End is all I want. When I've got the hotel up and running, maybe I'll think of settling down, if the right person comes along. But, I'm sorry, Alan,' her voice was gentle, 'you are not that person and never will be.'

'We'll see.' He leaned back. 'We'll see, Sarah. You'll change your mind eventually.'

Sarah sighed in exasperation. It was hopeless!

'Anyway,' Alan continued, 'there was

another reason for coming down today. Has Davinia told you?'

'You want to book Rainbow's End for a conference?'

Alan nodded. 'Eight solicitors, for three days. We have a conference once a year to discuss business and various other things.'

'That doesn't seem many people for a conference.'

'It's just a small private party. Mostly solicitors I qualified with, who have practises in the same area. We have a get together once a year.'

'A solicitors reunion,' Sarah commented dryly.

Alan smiled. 'Can you accommodate us?'

'When?'

'The first week in August.'

Sarah thought for a moment. 'Would they share? We have four double rooms you could have, that would leave me a family room free and one single.'

'That would be fine, I'm sure they'll agree.'

'Good,' said Sarah briskly. 'Then I'll go and enter a provisional booking and you can confirm when you return. When are you returning?' Sarah looking at Alan hopefully.

'We thought we'd stay until the end of the week, if that's all right. I'd like to have a look around, get my bearings, and your mother wants to spend some time with you.'

'Fine.' Sarah sighed. 'I'll go and sort things out with Molly. Jed will show you to your room.'

Alan frowned. 'I think I can find my own way.'

Sarah smiled. 'Room three, Alan. Up the stairs, second door on the left.'

★　★　★

Having sorted the extra guests with Molly she returned to her office. Paperwork wouldn't wait.

She wanted to go and explain her position with Alan to Jed, but, knowing Jed, she felt it prudent to wait until his anger cooled.

First Lucy and now Alan. People were so complicated!

She spent a moment dwelling on the fact that Lucy was Jed's sister and wondered what trouble she was in and then resolutely applied herself to the mail.

When Sarah went into the dining-room at lunchtime, she was surprised to see her mother sharing a table with Peter Ratton.

'Sarah, come and join us.' Her mother had obviously regained her good humour and was dressed in a glamorous silk dress that could have easily graced any elite London restaurant.

Sarah smiled at Peter and ordered soup and a roll from the young waitress. 'I don't normally stop for lunch,' she confided. 'But, just today, I'll make an exception.'

'Peter tells me he's staying,' her mother purred.

Sarah laughed. 'At least we have one

permanent booking! But there's a family arriving at the end of the month and we're getting walkers and weekenders in between, so business is looking up slowly. And of course,' she cast her mother a sideways glance, 'Alan's booked eight in for three days. So that will keep us busy.'

'I'm so glad, dear.' Her mother covered Sarah's hand with her own. 'I do want you to make a success of this. Peter tells me the food is delicious.'

Sarah cast him a grateful look as she sampled her own bowl of soup. It was indeed good. Molly was proving an accomplished cook. She only hoped she'd be able to find extra staff for when the conference was on.

She must call and see Mrs Williams and find out if any interest had been shown in the vacancy.

'Peter's been telling me all about the wonderful wildlife on the cliffs.' Her mother touched Peter's arm. 'And the gulls, so many varieties apparently. He's taking me for a walk this afternoon, to show me some of the species.'

'I hope you've brought some sensible shoes, mother.' Sarah suppressed a smile. 'Walking on the cliff tops can be hazardous.'

'Of course,' Davinia answered indignantly. 'I've got some lovely comfortable flatties. Just made for walking.'

'Then I wish you both a pleasant afternoon.'

She left them in the hall and couldn't resist smiling as she saw them set out.

Sarah crossed the yard and was pleased to see Jed by the gate. 'Jed,' she called. 'I need to talk to you.'

Jed's expression was cool as he watched her approach. Aloof, was the word, Sarah decided and put on her brightest smile.

'I'm sorry about this morning, Jed. You'll have to excuse Alan, an old friend who won't take 'no' for an answer.'

Jed remained silent and Sarah stood uncomfortably in front of him. 'Alan and I grew up together.' She felt she had to make Jed understand and was annoyed, with herself and with him. 'He always hoped we would make a couple, but I've never given him any encouragement, and he's certainly not my fiancé, and never likely to be.'

'It's none of my business.' Jed obviously wasn't convinced. 'Now,' his voice was cool, 'the lorry's arriving shortly with the tables and playground. Do you have any preference to layout?'

Sarah shook her head. 'I'll leave it all up to you, Jed. Space it in the orchard as you think fit. I'll come and have a look at it this evening.'

They parted formally and Sarah returned to the kitchen with a heavy heart. 'Molly,' she said in exasperation, 'why are men so infuriating?'

She stacked dishes in the dishwasher and Molly smiled, noting as she glanced out of the window Jed's receding back. Those two wanted their heads banging together!

She was very fond of Sarah and she wanted to see her happy. She thought

Rainbow's End was brilliant, but if it was Jed that would put the smile on her employer's face than she would have to do something about it!

But there was another matter on her mind as well. She had been speaking to Susan in the village that morning, and they had agreed that Sarah was entitled to the truth about her father. But how? She didn't want Sarah hurt. It was a problem.

⋆   ⋆   ⋆

Sarah enjoyed her mother's visit, although she saw little of her, her time being taken up with Peter and his wildlife booklet. Sarah had to smile. An interest in wildlife was the one thing her mother had never professed, but then, Peter had never been around before.

Alan had also remained out of her way, taking trips into Tremaine and around the area and for this she was grateful. She was even more grateful when she waved the pair off on the Friday and she felt herself relax.

Jed himself remained uncommunicative but, for the time being, she shelved her personal problems and concentrated on the business, trying desperately to forget their kiss on the boat. The daytime was busy, but in the night their romantic embrace came back to haunt her and her heart refused to dismiss Jed.

Her mother and Alan having departed for London, she set off for Tremaine and shopping. Entering the Stores she saw Mrs Williams was alone behind the counter.

'Any luck with my advert, Mrs Williams?' Sarah smiled at the elderly woman.

'I thought you'd got someone.' Mrs Williams looked startled.

'Got someone? Whatever do you mean?'

Mrs Williams looked flustered. 'Well, your young man came in on Wednesday. Said as how you'd found someone for the job and to take the advert down!'

'My young man?' Sarah was stupefied.

'Dark young man, said he was your fiancé, and was helping with the business.' Mrs Williams looked worried. 'Isn't that right?'

Alan, Alan had had cancelled her advert. What was he playing at? 'No, Mrs Williams, that is not right.' Sarah felt fury sweep through her and Mrs Williams looked alarmed.

'I'm sorry.' Sarah passed a hand through her hair. The whole situation was crazy. 'I know who you mean. He's a friend of my mother's and stayed for a few days. But, he's not helping me with my business and he is not my fiancé!'

'Some friend!' Mrs Williams muttered and leaned on the counter. 'I'm sorry, my dear.' She sounded distressed. 'I didn't know.'

'Of course not, how could you know.'

'I'll only take orders from you in future.' Mrs Williams looked cross.

'Silly man! Does that mean you're still wanting someone?'

'Indeed I am and pretty urgently. We've guests arriving tomorrow and Molly desperately needs help in the kitchen.'

Mrs Williams face cleared and she beamed at Sarah. 'Then there's no problem. Young Jennifer from down the village wants holiday work and she's a dab hand in the kitchen.

'Worked in the Grand Hotel last summer and she was asking about your job. I'll get on to her right away and send her up this afternoon. Is that all right?' She looked at Sarah anxiously.

'That's wonderful,' Sarah said fervently. 'She sounds great. Tell her to ask for me.'

'I'll tell her 'no-one else',' said Mrs Williams forcefully. 'Just you. She's not to speak to anyone else.'

Sarah smiled at her vehemence. 'That's fine,' she said and turned to go as the door opened.

A lady with a smiling face, but

anxious eyes, entered. Her pretty features were hardly diminished by age and her grey hair curled naturally to her shoulders.

'Susan,' Mrs Williams greeted the newcomer, 'have you met Sarah, who's bought Rainbow's End?'

She was staring at Susan rather pointedly and Susan studied the older woman. 'Susan's parents used to own the Stores,' Mrs Williams explained to Sarah, 'before me and my Alfie took it on.'

'I see.' Sarah smiled at Susan who had paled and was staring at her. 'Do I know you?' She hesitated and took a step forward as Susan remained silent.

Susan shook her head, her eyes never leaving Sarah's face.

'So you're Sarah, Roger's child,' she whispered.

'You knew my father?' Sarah was startled.

Susan nodded. 'When we were children.' She bit her lip and turned away. 'I've come for the papers, Annie.'

'Of course.' Mrs Williams dived under the counter and brought out a roll of newspapers. 'They're all here, Susan.'

The tension in the air was tangible. 'I'd like to talk to you sometime, about my father.' Sarah tentatively touched Susan's arm, and the older woman turned and looked at her.

Her eyes were sad. 'Of course,' she said. 'Sometime.'

The doorbell chimed and Sarah stood there, immobile. Mrs Williams muttered something about the phone ringing and disappeared into the back of the shop. Sarah was alone with her thoughts and, very slowly, she made her way back to Rainbow's End.

6

The next week the Fieldings arrived. A young couple with an adorable boy aged about five.

'And what's your name?' Sarah was booking the family in and waiting for Jed to take the suitcases to their room.

'Danny.' He gazed at her solemnly, large blue eyes framed by blond curls.

'Danny, that's nice.' Sarah smiled at his mother. 'What are you going to do on your holidays, Danny?'

'I want to go fishing,' he answered firmly.

'Now, Danny, we'll have to see, won't we.' His mother smiled apologetically at Sarah. 'He's fishing mad, ever since his uncle took him out in a rowboat and they caught tiddlers!'

Sarah laughed. 'Well, we'll see what we can arrange. In the meantime, there's climbing ropes and swings in the orchard . . . ' Jed appeared at her elbow. 'But we'll get you settled into your room first and then you can come and have a cup of tea and a piece of cake. How does that sound?'

'Wonderful.' Mr Fielding looked tired.

Jed picked up the cases and Sarah watched the small family mounting the stairs. One day she wanted a child like Danny, but she needed to find the right man first! Shaking off her feeling of despondency she completed the paper-work.

Jed was smiling when he came down the stairs. 'I've been booked for a fishing expedition.' He laughed. 'Seems young Danny isn't going to give his parents any peace until he's been fishing!'

'Is it safe?' Sarah saw Jed's eyes narrow and blushed.

'Of course,' he answered shortly. 'I've lifejackets and all the necessary equip-ment. I'm sure there'll be no problem, unless you've any objection?'

'No, of course not. I was just thinking of young Danny.'

'He'll have a lifejacket and I'll attach a harness rope to him. Don't worry, I won't let him fall overboard!' His voice was sarcastic and Sarah turned away, fuming.

Ever since their trip in the boat he had maintained a cool distance and, even though she had insisted that Alan was in no way betrothed to her, the easy familiarity between them had not returned.

The next day dawned clear and calm, balmy breezes gently curling the waves and Sarah saw the Fieldings set off on their fishing trip with some envy.

'Will Jed be doing many fishing trips?' Molly was mixing pastry.

'I don't know. Why?'

Sarah was lending a hand in the kitchen. Jennifer had proved an excellent choice by Mrs Williams, but she was unable to start until the next day.

'Well,' Molly hesitated, 'it's none of my business really. But most of the fishing trips are done by David, from Stoney Cottage.' She looked sideways at Sarah. 'He's a fisherman as well, but fish stocks being what they are, he relies on tourist trips to boost his income. Course, I don't suppose Jed knew that.' Her fingers moved quickly in the mix.

'Well, no,' Sarah said thoughtfully. 'I mean, he only agreed to take young Danny out as a favour. He's not charging. And he won't be able to do it regularly, I need him here.'

Molly nodded, apparently satisfied. 'It doesn't do to upset the locals,' she commented brusquely.

'I have no intention of upsetting the locals! Surely one little fishing trip can't do that?'

'No, I expect not.'

'Don't forget, Molly, my father was a local here too.'

'Did he never tell you anything about Tremaine?' Molly floured a board and turned the pastry out for rolling. She still found this difficult to believe.

'Never. The first Mum and I heard

about it was after he died. His birth certificate and various other childhood documents came to life and we realised that Tremaine was his birthplace. Why he never mentioned it I don't know because most people seem to remember him. It's very puzzling.'

'Hmm.' Molly rolled the pastry.

'I mean,' Sarah turned from the sink, 'you knew him, Molly. Why didn't he tell us about his home?'

Molly shrugged but didn't comment.

'I suppose,' Sarah said reflectively, 'it had been a good few years since he left and he'd settled in the city. Then of course he met Mum and their life centred on London. When you're young, roots aren't that important. I imagine he would have come back one day, only he didn't get the chance.' She sighed.

'So you came back instead?'

'I only meant to visit. See where he was born. But then I saw Rainbow's End and fell in love with it. And here I am! And I still haven't seen where he was actually born; it's been so busy. Will you take me, Molly?'

'The village has changed since he was a boy.' Molly's voice was gruff.

'Yes, well.' Sarah stared at her, wondering as she increasingly did so, why everyone seemed to remember her father, but no-one was prepared to talk about him. Even Molly, she was sure, was hiding something.

In Stoney Cottage a similar conversation was taking place. 'Now, David, calm down.' Susan put her arm around her agitated husband. 'Just because Jed's taken some of Sarah's guests on a fishing trip doesn't mean he's trying to knuckle in on your trade.'

'But what if he does? And he's not charging. Molly said . . .'

'Molly should have kept her mouth shut!' Susan said angrily. 'She wasn't thinking.'

'Yes, she was, she was thinking about us! This is our living we're talking about. And if word gets round that he's giving trips for nothing, then folks won't be paying for the likes of me!'

'Jed is employed as a handyman. I'm sure he isn't going to have the time to be taking folks out. You mark my words, he'll do the odd trip as a favour for Sarah's guests and that'll be that.'

She looked at her husband worriedly. The doctor had said categorically he had to avoid stress and heaven knew there had been enough of that lately. What with Roger's girl moving in and now this.

How was she supposed to keep her husband stress free? She was feeling pretty stressed herself and she didn't like the situation not one bit!

'Molly will keep us informed,' she said soothingly.

'And what about the fish?'

'Oh, for goodness sake, David, what on earth difference is a few mackerel going to make. Have some sense, do!'

She turned away irritably and her husband sighed. 'I'm sorry, Susan.' He reached his hand towards her. 'I'm sorry. I'm just upset, that's all. First Roger and now Sarah here, I just don't know what to do.'

'You don't have to do anything, my love.' Susan put her arm round her husband's shoulder and he leaned against her.

'I don't deserve you. I've brought you nothing but trouble.'

'Don't you ever say that!' Susan spoke fiercely. 'I love you, always have. We've had a good marriage and one little bit of trouble isn't going to alter that.'

'Really?' He smiled tentatively up at her.

'Really.' She kissed him gently. 'I've never regretted marrying you, David, and just you remember that.'

David took her hand and kissed it. 'Thank you, sweetheart. I just feel so useless lately, since I've been ill. And this business does worry me.'

'There, love, don't fret, it'll all sort out in the wind.' Susan patted her husband on the arm and went to make tea, hoping her prophecy would come true.

But for the life of her she couldn't see an answer to the dilemma at that moment. She knew in her heart she would have to take courage in both hands and go and visit Sarah, but, each day, she baulked at the idea. 'I'll go tomorrow,' she would mutter, but the tomorrows were running out and eventually Sarah would be knocking on her door, the truth learned from someone else. And she didn't want that.

At Rainbow's End the Fieldings returned from their trip happy and hungry. Danny was overjoyed with the mackerel, the soggy bag clutched in his grubby hands and he went off excitedly to present them to Molly.

'I'm sure Molly will cook them for your tea,' Sarah said solemnly and crossed her fingers that Molly would agree.

'Now, Danny,' his mother was smiling, 'upstairs with you and a good scrub to get rid of that fishy smell.'

Danny bounced gleefully away and, after thanking Sarah, his parents followed suit. There was no sign of Jed.

The mackerel were duly demolished and the tables cleared. As the sun began setting over the calm water Sarah made herself a cup of coffee and settled into her armchair. She felt tired. She could see the gulls wheeling over the sea wall and the faint splash of the incoming tide on the shingle drifted in through the open window.

Across the yard she saw Jed lock the sheds for the night and walk slowly through the back gate to the orchard. She longed to go to him and try to mend the tension between them but she didn't have the energy. Bridge building would have to wait till the morrow.

Suddenly, an agitated knocking on her door interrupted her. It was Molly, her face anxious.

'Sorry, Sarah. But I was just leaving and there was this man at the front door.' Molly twisted her hands together. 'He's wanting to see Jed, but I don't like the looks of him, so I thought I'd better have a word with you first.'

'What's the matter with him?'

'Well, he wasn't very polite. And when I said we were closed for the night, he said he'd wait on the doorstep till morning!'

'All right, Molly. You get off home. I'll come and see what he wants.'

'Are you sure it's wise, by yourself? Perhaps you'd better fetch Jed, just in case.'

'Let's go and see.'

Sarah followed Molly through the hall and there, standing determinedly on the doorstep, a bulging briefcase in his hand, was a short, rotund man, a grim expression on his face.

'Can I help you, Mr . . . ?' Sarah waited as the dark suited man eyed her from top to toe.

'You own this hotel?' His voice was cultured, but hard.

She nodded. 'What can I do for you?' Sarah repeated, glad that Molly was still hovering in the background. She had to agree with Molly. She didn't care for his aggressive attitude at all.

'Do you employ a man called Jed Danielle?' Sarah wasn't sure how to answer that one. She employed a Jed certainly, but his surname had never been mentioned.

But she could hardly admit to having an employee whose surname was unknown.

'What do you want to know for?' She decided that attack was the best line of defence.

'Well,' the man hesitated, 'it's not actually him I'm looking for. It's his sister, Lucy. She's the one I've been told to find,' he said darkly.

'I definitely don't employ anyone called Lucy,' Sarah said in a firm voice. 'So I suggest you get off my doorstep and return from whence you came.'

There were footsteps behind her and Sarah turned to see Molly, an apologetic look on her face. She was followed by Jed.

'I didn't like the way things were

going,' Molly whispered and Sarah had to admit to a feeling of relief.

'What's going on?' Jed towered in the doorway, his lips compressed.

The man sighed in defeat. 'I'm looking for Lucy Danielle,' he repeated, his voice gloomy. 'Been told to serve these papers on her. But I can't find her and the only name I got in the village was Jed Danielle, her brother.'

'Well, you've found him.' Jed snatched the papers from the man's hand.

'Give them back.' The man was gesticulating wildly. 'I'm supposed to give them to Lucy.'

'I'll see she gets them.' Jed's voice was grim. 'Now, are you leaving or shall I call the police?'

The man backed away from the door. 'I'm leaving,' he said angrily. 'But you'll be hearing from us further. You've no right . . .'

'Goodnight.' Jed slammed the door and they watched through the window as the man walked quickly away, his briefcase waving about in anger.

Sarah and Molly heaved a sight of relief. 'Thanks, Jed.'

'You should have fetched me straight away.' Jed glared at Sarah. 'This is my business.'

'It becomes my business when it arrives on the doorstep of Rainbow's End.' Sarah's shock was turning to anger and then she checked herself as she noticed Molly, wide-eyed, taking in every word.

'Thanks for your help, Molly. You can get off home now, you'll be late.'

'Yes, of course.' Molly sounded disappointed that she wasn't to know the reason for the late night call but she obediently trotted away down the drive. Sarah smiled. No doubt Molly's curiosity would have to be appeased in the morning, but now, she turned to Jed.

'What was all that about?'

Jed sighed. 'I'm sorry, Sarah, I shouldn't have brought my family problems on to your doorstep. That's why I took Lucy into Tremaine and rented Mrs Williams' flat for her. I thought she'd be out of harm's way until things were sorted out.'

'What things?'

'It's very complicated.' Jed was looking through the papers. 'It seems Lucy is being sued for breach of contract. Also that they're accusing her of . . . theft?'

'What?'

'Apparently the police are also after her. Good grief, what has she been up to? She didn't tell me any of this!'

'If it's true.'

'If it were true, the police would have been here already.' Jed looked thoughtful. 'There's something awfully fishy going on here.'

Sarah couldn't help smiling. A lot of things had been 'fishy' lately. But this appeared to be the worst.

'We'll sort it out in the morning,' Jed said wearily. 'When I've had time to read all this, and find out who that dumbo was in the first place. Whatever it's all about, Lucy is going to need a solicitor.'

'I know just the one! If you'll accept help from me that is?' She spoke tartly and Jed winced at the sharpness of her words.

'Of course I'll accept your help, Sarah.' His voice had gentled. 'I didn't want you involved, that's all. You've enough on your plate with Rainbow's End without taking on your employees' problems.'

'As I said,' Sarah replied, 'when it affects Rainbow's End then it becomes my problem.' Sarah locked the front door. 'We'll talk some more in the morning, when you've had a chance to read those documents. Whatever trouble Lucy is in its going to affect you, and therefore my hotel, until it's sorted. So my interest stands.'

Without further ado she bade Jed a stiff goodnight. But her sleep was disturbed with nightmares that involved a blond girl in a red T-shirt and a black suited Alan.

7

The next morning Sarah saw Jed crossing the yard, an absorbed expression on his face. She called from her open window. 'Jed, come in here a moment.'

Reluctantly Jed entered her office. 'I really don't want to involve you in my problems,' Jed protested again as Sarah waved him to a chair. He sat anyway.

'I'm already involved,' Sarah answered. 'Anyway, the sooner this matter is cleared up, the sooner I shall have your full attention back.'

Jed sighed and accepted the mug of coffee she handed to him.

'What I suggest,' Sarah seated herself behind her desk, 'is that we get Lucy up here. I take it you've read the papers?' Jed nodded.

'If she can come here this morning, we'll discuss the situation and I can give Alan a ring.' She saw Jed's frown.

'Alan, your fiancé.' He grimaced.

'Not my fiancé,' Sarah said determinedly. 'An old friend, and an excellent solicitor. I'm sure he'll take Lucy on and this whole mess can be cleared up.'

Jed shrugged. 'If you're positive?'

Accepting help from Sarah was obviously going against his principles, but Sarah ignored his ill-humour.

'I'm positive. Now,' she stood up, 'phone Lucy and we'll have a meeting at eleven. Then perhaps we can get on with normal work this afternoon.'

Jed nodded. 'She's renting the flat above the Stores. Mrs Williams seems to have taken her under her wing.' He sighed deeply. 'I'm sorry, Sarah.' He smiled slightly. 'I really didn't want to involve you.'

'Let's just get it sorted, shall we?' She opened the door and watched Jed as he disappeared down the hall. Sighing she went to see how Jennifer was faring in the kitchen with Molly on her first day.

At least she seemed to be getting the staff problem sorted!

★ ★ ★

Lucy arrived promptly at eleven, looking shamefaced. She didn't meet Sarah's eyes as she was led into the office and Sarah thought how vulnerable she looked now she no longer sported a red T-shirt!

Jed joined them and Lucy waited uneasily, shifting from one foot to another. Sarah judged her to be in her late teens although she could have passed for older.

'Let's sit down.' Sarah motioned to chairs and Jed sat, the sheaf of papers on his lap. 'Perhaps you'd like to explain the summons, Jed.' Sarah started the ball rolling.

'Well, as far as I can see,' Jed frowned at his sister, 'you signed an employment contract with this Mr Goode, and then walked out, taking a wardrobe full of expensive clothes with you. He's suing for breach of contract and the value of his clothes.'

'That's not true!' Lucy said.

'Did you sign a contract with him?'

'Well, yes. But he said the job was waiting on tables in his club. He said I would get a chance to sing when it was quiet. You know I've always wanted to be a singer.'

'And an actress, and a writer, and goodness knows what else. But I've seen very little sign of any training done for anything since you left school!' Jed sounded cross.

'I needed money to live,' Lucy pouted. 'And I wanted to enjoy myself for a while. That boarding school was horrid.'

'It gave you a good education, which seems to have been wasted.'

'What about you?' Lucy retaliated. 'You went to business school and you've ended up sweeping yards!'

'I'm not in trouble, Lucy.' Jed's voice was icy. 'Do you want me to phone Mum and Dad?'

Lucy shook her head and sank back in her chair. 'Anyway,' she continued. 'Bill promised he'd look after me and said that scouts often came to his club. If I was good enough one of them would spot me and I'd be on my way.'

'How gullible can you get?' Jed's voice rose in anger. 'For heaven's sake, Lucy, haven't I taught you anything? I suppose this Bill picked you up at some party or other and you trusted him, without checking anything out?'

Lucy looked mutinous. 'It was a very nice party, and he seemed a nice man.'

'Did you read the contract?' Lucy shook her head and Sarah could see tears forming in her eyes.

'Bill suddenly wasn't such a nice man after all.' Lucy shivered at the memory. 'I grabbed the first coat I came to and ran out the back door. I haven't seen Bill since.'

'That was when you came down here to me?' Jed asked.

Lucy nodded. 'I went back to my flat, packed my bags and headed for

Tremaine. I was afraid Bill would come looking for me, he knew where I lived, so I came to you.'

'As usual.' Jed sighed. 'Lucy, you really are going to have to start acting your age. What would Dad say, I really don't know.'

'Don't tell him,' Lucy begged.

'I can't at the moment,' Jed conceded. 'They're having a difficult time in Africa. He's got enough to worry about without a wayward teenager.'

'I promise I'll behave in future.' Lucy brightened. 'I like the flat at Mrs Williams' and I've got a part time job.'

'You have?'

'In the art shop, with Sebastian. He's taken me on to help out during the summer.'

'Good grief!' Sarah stared at her. 'You're working for Sebastian?'

Lucy nodded and smiled. 'I gather you know him. He's asked me all sorts of questions about you.'

'He has?' Sarah frowned. 'What sort of questions?'

'About your background. Of course I don't know anything much, so I couldn't tell him. But he gave me a job anyway.'

Jed sighed. 'Does he know about your trouble?' Lucy shook her head. 'Poor Sebastian,' Jed muttered. 'He didn't realise what he was taking on!'

Lucy looked crestfallen. 'What am I going to do, Jed?' she whispered.

Sarah intervened. 'The first thing I'm going to do is phone Alan, he's a friend of mine.' She smiled at Lucy ignoring Jed's sudden frown. 'He's a solicitor and I'm sure he'll help.'

Lucy brightened as Sarah picked up the phone. She got straight through to Alan.

'Alan,' she kept her voice light, 'I'm returning the favour of the conference, I've found you a client.'

'I'm rather busy at the moment, Sarah.' Alan's voice was cool. 'What's the problem?'

'I've a young lady with me by the name of Lucy. She's got herself into a contractual dispute with an unsavoury character called Bill Goode. He runs a club in London. I thought you might help her out?'

'What's she doing with you?'

'She came to her brother, Jed, for help, and I thought of you.'

'Jed's sister?' Alan's voice was thoughtful. 'Well, in that case . . . ' He was silent for a moment. 'Yes, in that case I may be able to fit her in. Can she come up to London?'

'She'll be on the next train,' Sarah said. 'I'll book her into a guesthouse and she could come and see you in the morning if you have an appointment free?'

'Ten o'clock?'

'That's wonderful. Thanks Alan. See you at the conference next week.'

The line went dead and Sarah smiled at Lucy. 'There you are, Lucy. I'll give you a map to show you where Alan's office is. I know a good guesthouse not far away. Now, all you have to do is get yourself there.'

'What about Sebastian?'

'Tell him you need a couple of days off,' Jed said. 'And get yourself to London! Be thankful that Sarah was able to help.'

'Oh, I am.' Lucy smiled. 'Thank you Sarah, so much. I promise, when this is sorted out, I'll never get into trouble again.'

'We'll see!' Jed muttered and followed Lucy out of the office.

★　★　★

The next morning, her paperwork done, she wandered round into the orchard. She had been pleased to receive two more family bookings for the week and the conference and the hikers had phoned to say there were on their return journey and wanted rooms for two nights. Rainbow's End was filling up.

She noticed Danny climbing the adventure frame Jed had constructed in the far corner, where the noise of excited children would be swallowed up in the mountains that towered behind the stone wall, and Danny's father was seated at one of the wooden tables, placed comfortably under a tree, where he could keep an eye on his son.

He was reading a paper and Sarah noticed how his face had filled out and relaxed since the family had arrived. Jed was scything grass around Cynthia and stopped as she approached.

'I wondered if you'd heard from Lucy?' Sarah hesitated.

'Come and sit down.' Jed pulled a chair on to the newly-cut grass. 'Coffee?'

She watched young Danny trying daring feats on the ropes and smiled as Jed sat with her. 'Lovely child,' she commented. 'You've done an excellent job with the orchard, Jed. It looks super and the adventure frame is obviously a success.'

'Lucy phoned this morning.' Jed went on. 'She's seen Alan and he thinks he can extricate her from her contract. Bill

Goode is a well-known thug, he enjoys bullying the vulnerable. But Alan thinks he'll release Lucy without payment. He won't want the trouble of a court case. And Lucy's returned the coat she borrowed.'

'Thank goodness for that!' Sarah breathed a sigh of relief.

'I must say thank you, Sarah, and I'm sorry for my grumpiness.'

Sarah accepted the apology eagerly. More than anything she wanted to be back on friendly terms with Jed. She realised how much a part of her life he had become. She needed him and not just for the business.

'Is Lucy coming back?'

Jed nodded. 'She hopes to be back at the end of the week. Perhaps then she'll buckle down and do something with her life.'

They sat quietly for a while, basking in the warm sunshine and a feeling of utter contentment seeped into Sarah. 'Ah, this is lovely,' she breathed.

Jed looked at her and she felt herself

colour at the intensity of his scrutiny. Her heart started to pound and she felt suddenly nervous.

'You're really not engaged to Alan?' Jed asked quietly.

'No. Definitely not.' Sarah dropped her eyes. 'He's the son of a friend of my mother. The mothers have always hoped . . . And I know Alan seems to have got the idea we were made for each other. But I've never thought of him in that way, and never will.'

'I'm glad.' Jed was watching her, the expression tender and Sarah felt hope well in her heart.

★ ★ ★

The next day brought a call from Davinia. 'I'm on my way, darling. Be with you in a couple of hours. Just wanted to make sure you'd be there to greet me. Is there a room free?'

Sarah sighed. 'Of course, mother. I'll have it made up straight away. Safe journey.'

Davinia arrived after lunch looking as elegant as ever and calling for Jed to unload her large suitcase.

'How long are you staying?' Sarah eyed the case suspiciously.

'Oh, a while.' Davinia waved her arm vaguely. 'I thought I might help with Alan's conference, and of course I wanted to see you were all right. You looked decidedly peaky last time I arrived.'

As Sarah had just emerged from the depths of the sea, she thought 'peaky' was hardly the word, but she didn't comment.

'Number Three, please Jed.' She grinned at Jed who was disengaging himself from her mother's vociferous welcome.

'Now then, Davinia, let's get upstairs and you can tell me all your news.' Jed picked up the case.

'What an offer!' Davinia simpered and picked up her handbag. 'Oh, by the way,' Davinia called in a casual voice over her shoulder, 'where's the delicious Peter?'

Sarah smiled. 'Out on one of his rambles I think.'

Davinia looked crestfallen. 'Oh.' Then she brightened. 'Oh well, he'll be back for dinner I expect. Time for me to freshen up.' And she trotted gaily after Jed as he disappeared up the stairs.

Sarah looked thoughtful as she went to the kitchen to tell Molly there would be one extra for dinner. She hoped her mother wouldn't upset Peter Ratton in any way. Peter was a likeable chap, and he was only just getting over the death of his wife. He would be vulnerable. But he was also sensible, Sarah reminded herself, and probably her mother's bright company would help him feel less lonely.

The evening meal disposed of, Molly served coffees in the lounge and Sarah noticed her mother and Peter in deep conversation at one of the small tables.

Peter had drawings and papers spread out and Davinia was showing absorbed interest. Molly chuckled as they returned to the kitchen.

The doorbell chimed. 'Are you expecting guests?' Molly looked startled and Sarah shook her head. It was half-past eight and no-one was booked in until Saturday.

'I'll go and see.' Sarah sighed as she approached the door. She hoped it wasn't that horrible little man back looking for Lucy.

She opened the front door. 'Hello, Sarah.' Alan's voice was bright and he was grinning.

'I'm sorry we didn't ring, but spur of the moment, you know. I'm sure you can put us up.'

'Alan, what are you doing here?' Sarah was nonplussed.

'Lucy was coming home, nearly sorted her out. And then I thought, why not? I'd drive her down, and come and check out the arrangements for the conference. Didn't intend to be so late, but by the time I'd dropped Lucy off at her flat . . . Anyway here I am. You have got rooms free?'

'Well, it will have to be one of the double rooms. Mother's here as well.'

'Davinia? How marvellous.'

Sarah frowned. 'You said rooms? You haven't brought the rest of the conference with you as well, have you?'

Alan laughed. 'No, no way. They're arriving on Saturday as planned. No.' He turned to look towards his car. 'I've brought a friend with me. She particularly asked to come to Rainbow's End.'

Sarah watched as an elegant woman emerged from the car. Dressed immaculately and wearing an astonishing hat, she almost put Davinia in the shade. She glided to the door balancing on pin-thin heels and held out her hand.

'Sarah. I'm Marcia. I've heard so much about you.' Her voice was husky and Sarah watched her, mesmerised.

'You want a room?' Sarah managed to croak.

Marcia laughed a tinkling laugh. 'I hope not.' She was obviously enjoying

Sarah's reaction. 'No, I'm looking for Jed. Alan tells me he's living here.' She smiled seductively into Sarah's astonished face. 'If you'd just let him know I'm here.'

8

'You'll find Jed behind the hotel, in the orchard.' Sarah found her voice although she felt anger course through her at Marcia's appearance and Alan's grinning face.

'In the orchard?' Marcia's face was a picture and Sarah felt a grin surface. She looked at Marcia's shoes and then pointed to the lane that ran along the side of the house.

'You go up there,' she waved in the general direction, 'it leads to the orchard. You'll find Jed in a caravan in the corner.'

'In a caravan?' Marcia's look of horror was mounting and she cast Alan a furious look. 'You mean he's not staying in the hotel?'

Sarah raised her eyebrows as haughtily as she could. 'Of course not! Perhaps you'd escort her round, Alan?'

Alan was beginning to look distinctly uncomfortable. Whether or not he realised Jed slept in a caravan Sarah wasn't sure, but he obviously hadn't conveyed that fact to Marcia. Although, Sarah conceded to herself, if Marcia had known she probably wouldn't have come.

'I'll have your room made up, Alan. When you've taken Marcia to Jed, come in through the back door and I'll give you the key.'

Then she frowned. Molly, who had been hovering in the background, looked at her expectantly. 'Sorry, Molly, but can you make up the bed in room five? Alan will have to have one of the double rooms for now; he was going to share for the conference anyway.'

'On my way.' Molly bustled away and Sarah sighed despondently. Who on earth was Marcia? She wondered if she'd ever get to know Jed and his secrets. Just when things were going so well between them again, now this!

Ah well, she headed for the kitchen.

No doubt Alan would want a drink and a sandwich so she'd better be prepared.

It wasn't long before a trio appeared at the back door. Alan looked flustered and extremely red in the face, Marcia furious and Jed marched in front of them both, stern faced.

'Sarah?' Jed called, his voice thunderous. Sarah surveyed the angry group.

'Yes, Jed?' She smiled sweetly.

Jed glowered at her. 'I believe you have a room prepared for Alan. Is it possible to prepare one for Marcia?'

'Of course, Jed. It's already done. Show her up to room six please.'

Jed picked up the suitcase and stormed up the stairs without further ado. Marcia managed a weak smile and followed him meekly. Alan ignored Sarah completely and carried his own case behind them.

'There's coffee and sandwiches in the lounge,' Sarah called after them and disappeared into the kitchen, a smile on her face.

As it was, the coffee and sandwiches

remained untouched. She saw neither of her unexpected guests again that evening and somehow Jed managed to sneak back to his caravan without her noticing.

The next day dawned bright and sunny. Alan appeared in her office after breakfast, looking rather shame-faced.

'Did you sleep well?' Sarah smiled brightly.

He nodded. 'I shan't be staying,' he announced coldly.

'What a shame!' Sarah couldn't keep the glee out of her voice. 'And Marcia?'

'I'm taking her back to town.' Alan's face reddened slightly and he glared at Sarah. 'I was misled in my information.'

'How difficult for a solicitor,' Sarah murmured.

'I'll be back on Saturday with the others for the conference. I take it everything will be ready?'

'Of course,' Sarah answered smoothly. 'How is the case with Lucy?'

'Nearly concluded. I don't think there'll be any more problems with Bill

Goode. Just a few loose ends to tie up and Lucy will be in the clear.'

'Thanks, Alan. I do appreciate your taking her case on.'

He shrugged. 'It wasn't too difficult. I'll be sending my bill to Jed.'

'Of course.' Sarah studied Alan. She wondered what had induced him to arrive with Marcia in the first place. Taking the plunge she asked him.

He looked uncomfortable. 'Lucy informed me Jed was engaged to Marcia. I happened to know her father, got in touch and apparently Marcia had been scouring the country for him. It appears there had been a lovers' tiff and Jed had walked out. She had been trying to contact him ever since. It seemed an ideal way to bring the lovers together.'

Alan didn't quite meet Sarah's eyes and she knew he had had an ulterior motive for his actions. But she could hardly accuse him of being jealous of Jed!

'But apparently the lovers don't want

to be together?' Sarah persisted.

Alan shook his head. 'Apparently not.' He spoke crossly. 'Jed made that quite plain.' He shifted uncomfortably. 'Marcia's terribly upset.'

'Perhaps arriving unannounced was not the best way to approach Jed,' Sarah suggested. 'A phone call or a letter first might not have come amiss.'

He left the office and Sarah heaved a sigh of relief. She had no wish to meet Marcia again, so remained engrossed in her paperwork until she was sure they had departed.

Her mother found her there. 'Was that Alan I saw in the hall?'

'It was,' Sarah replied. 'He was checking on the arrangements for tomorrow.'

'But he's gone?' Davinia looked perplexed.

Sarah nodded. 'He'll be back tomorrow, with his cronies.' She had no intention of explaining about Marcia. 'You can go through the arrangements with me this afternoon if you like,

Mum. You know Alan's requirements better than I.'

'When I get back.' Her mother blushed. 'Peter's taking me out to lunch, but we'll be back around mid afternoon and I'll check everything then.'

That evening Sarah could contain her curiosity no longer. She approached Jed in the orchard. He was making a second swing.

'Jed.' Sarah stood and watched his strong hands twining the rope. He grunted, engrossed in his task. 'Marcia's gone.' She waited for his reaction.

He turned and looked at her. 'So?'

She blushed. 'I hope her arrival didn't cause too many problems?'

He shrugged and tested the swing with his weight. 'That should be OK.' He gathered up his tools. 'Do you want a drink?' He headed back to Cynthia without waiting for her reply.

'Thanks.'

He fetched two glasses of wine and they sat for a moment in silence.

'I take it Lucy told Alan about Marcia?' She spoke tentatively.

'I expect.' His face was thunderous.

'She wasn't to know.'

He sighed. 'Lucy always brings trouble! But it wasn't her fault.'

Sarah waited. Jed stretched his legs in front of him and let out another sigh. 'When I left business college, I was taken on by her father, a financial adviser. Somehow Marcia and I became engaged. Then I decided it was not what I wanted and we had a row. End of story!'

'I see.' Sarah looked at him thoughtfully. 'And is it still not what you want?'

'Decidedly. I'm sick of women mucking up my life! All I want is peace and quiet, my two Cynthias and a life that's love free.'

'So you no longer love Marcia?'

'I never did.'

'So why did you get engaged?'

Jed shrugged. 'Heaven knows! I'm not sure how it happened.'

'So you weren't there at the time?'

Sarah's voice was sarcastic.

'Of course I was!' Jed turned towards her, anger making his voice harsh. 'Anyway, it's none of your business.'

'Your business seems to keep arriving on my doorstep,' Sarah retorted. 'So that makes it my business.'

'I'd best be moving on then.' Jed was in a foul mood.

'You please yourself!' Sarah was stung to report. She stood up. 'I wouldn't want you staying here against your will.'

He stared at the new swing, swaying slightly in the breeze and Sarah turned away. There was no point talking to Jed in this mood; she was only making matters worse. She'd apologise in the morning when he'd calmed down. And he was right; it was none of her business.

Brushing the tears angrily from her cheeks she went to bed, but her sleep was disturbed and she awoke heavy-eyed the next morning.

At ten o'clock precisely, two smart

BMWs rolled up in front of the door. Eight dark suited solicitors emerged and surveyed the scene.

Alan approached her smirking. 'Sarah, these are my colleagues. Perhaps you could get your man to show them to their rooms?'

Jed appeared on cue and, other than a brief nod in Sarah's direction, he didn't communicate. The solicitors followed him up the stairs, but Sarah could hear their grumbling comments as they disappeared from view and a worried frown creased her brow.

Having settled, the group took off in their cars for Tremaine and Sarah looked in annoyance at the spurted gravel. These were not the sort of guests she had hoped to encourage, but at least the rooms were all practically full.

Trouble started at dinner that night. The men had drunk several bottles of wine before the meal was served and she saw them push the roast beef and vegetables around their plates as

Jennifer served up.

'What's this, Alan?' The man's voice was loud and insulting. 'I thought you said the food was cordon bleu and excellent?'

Alan had an innocent expression on his face and suddenly Sarah's heart sank. She could feel the tension in the dining-room and the Fieldings were watching anxiously.

'I'm sure Sarah will do better tomorrow.' Alan's voice was soothing and she was horrified by his grin of triumph. 'Won't you, Sarah?'

'Of course,' Sarah spoke smoothly. 'If the food is not to your liking I'm sure we can arrange to change the meals for you. I wasn't given any instructions, so served our usual menu.' She was passing through the tables, filling wine glasses.

'Where's the cabaret then?' Another voice chimed above the conversation.

'Cabaret?' Sarah paused. 'What cabaret?'

'There's no entertainment?' The

man's voice became belligerent. 'Alan, you said . . . '

'Alan seems to have said an awful lot!' she muttered to herself as she returned to the kitchen.

'We've got problems, Molly,' she said wearily as she sank on to a stool. 'I'm not sure how to sort this one out.'

'Fetch your mother down,' Molly said immediately. 'She works wonders.'

Davinia listened to Sarah's explanation with a frown on her face. 'Are you sure Alan has said all these things?' She sounded doubtful. 'I mean, he's trying to help you. He wouldn't have misinformed his friends, surely?'

'He would.' Sarah brushed her hair back wearily. 'He would, if he wanted me to make a mess of running Rainbow's End. One disastrous conference, word gets around, and I haven't even got off the ground yet!'

'I'll speak to him,' Davinia said. But when Davinia and Sarah went downstairs they found the solicitors had gone into Tremaine.

* ★ ★ ★

The next morning saw the group picking at their bacon and egg. None of them looked very cheerful and Sarah smiled grimly. 'Serve them right,' she thought.

'What are we going to do this morning in this place?' one of the suits muttered.

'Heaven only knows!' his companion replied gloomily. 'Alan's got a lot to answer for. Where is he?'

'Still in bed.'

Breakfast complete the men mooched disconsolately around the lounge. 'I've got to do something,' Sarah muttered.

Davinia appeared. 'Is that them?' She gestured towards the lounge and Sarah nodded.

'Right.' Pulling her shoulders back Davinia swept into the room, her tinkling laugh and charming smile directed at the morose group. Before long laughter could be heard and Sarah breathed a sigh of relief. Thank goodness for her mother.

'We're going out for the day,' Davinia announced as she entered the kitchen. 'I'm taking the men on a guided tour. There's a wonderful leisure centre a few miles away, with all sorts of entertainment and I gather they also do a daytime show while you eat lunch. That should keep them happy.'

'Mum, you're an angel.' Sarah kissed her mother.

'Can you do something about the evening meal?' Davinia whispered to Sarah, not wanting to upset Molly. 'Something a bit exotic? And I'll try and arrange tonight's jollities while we're out. Tomorrow they'll be on their way home.'

'Is Alan coming with you?'

'He hasn't surfaced yet, so we're leaving him behind,' Davinia said complacently. 'I think that way we'll avoid any confrontation. They're a nice bunch really. Rainbow's End just isn't what Alan led them to believe, that's all.'

Molly was very huffy over the fact that her dinners were not appreciated. 'All I know is plain cooking. It's been good enough for everyone else.'

'Of course it has, Molly. I'm not complaining. But we can't let Alan get the better of us, can we?' Sarah cajoled. 'Let's surprise him and produce something they'll enjoy!'

At that moment Jed opened the kitchen door. He ignored Sarah completely and asked Molly for a coffee. Molly banged the kettle and proceeded to tell him about the difficult guests that had cast aspersions on her cooking.

'Your cooking is wonderful, Molly.' He smiled at the irate cook.

'They don't think so!' She slammed a mug on to the table.

'The customer is always right?' He spoke gently.

'Hmm.' Molly shook out a teacloth. 'So what am I supposed to do?'

'Well,' Jed looked thoughtful, 'what was on the menu for tonight?'

'Pork,' Molly said firmly. 'With apple

sauce, potatoes and veg. Good enough for anyone.'

'How about dicing the pork, making a spicy sauce and serving with rice?' Jed suggested and Molly looked at him as if he'd gone mad.

'Oh Jed, you wouldn't help out, would you?' Sarah could see salvation at hand.

He turned cold eyes to her. 'I thought you could manage without me? I only came in to tell you I'd be leaving at the end of the week.'

Sarah bit her lip. 'Please, Jed. We're in an awful fix and I'm sure Molly would be grateful.'

Molly looked unsure about that, but stood, arms akimbo. 'I'll help Molly out certainly.' He emphasised the word Molly. 'I don't like to think of that creep getting the better of us. Between us, Molly, we can concoct a dinner that will leave them drooling!'

Molly sighed and smiled wryly. 'If you say so, Jed. But I don't like it. And we don't want any more of them sort of guests booking in.' She cast a baleful eye at Sarah and Sarah nodded meekly, deciding it was time she made an exit from the kitchen.

Jed to the rescue again. Was there no end to that man's talents? She wandered disconsolately around Rainbow's End, for once not getting the release from her unhappiness she usually got from her hotel. It was all so difficult. Not for the first time she wondered at her wisdom in taking this project on and, even more so, at her wisdom in employing Jed!

She heard nothing more from the kitchen, but the clatter of pans was promising and she hoped the men wouldn't stay out too late.

Alan was also making himself scarce. He hadn't been down for breakfast and she'd seen no sign of him.

Minutes before dinner was due to be served the BMWs finally rolled up the drive. The men were all laughing and looked as if they'd had a good day.

'I'll just go and tidy up,' Davinia

whispered. 'Super day, love, they're all as happy as can be. Fixed dinner?'

Sarah nodded and crossed her fingers. 'Should be exotic enough for them,' she whispered back. 'Oh, and Peter's waiting for you in the lounge.'

Her mother's face lit up and, with a wave of her hand, she mounted the stairs.

Suddenly the front door slammed open and Mr Fielding rushed in, his face filled with panic.

'Quickly, get help!'

'What's the matter?' Sarah took his hand. 'Tell me what's happened.'

'It's Danny,' Mr Fielding could hardly speak, 'he's been wanting to go fishing again. I thought he was on the beach, playing in the rock pools. Then I called and he didn't come.

Next thing I saw was Jed's boat, rolling over the waves. Danny was waving from the deck. I tried to reach him, but the tide carried him out. He's out there, alone on the sea. Dear God, please help!'

9

Davinia turned and Sarah sped into the kitchen. 'Jed, young Danny's released your boat. He's going out on the tide in Cynthia!'

'Good grief! How on earth . . . ?' Jed followed Sarah into the hall.

'Davinia,' Peter had arrived and took charge, 'go and help Molly with the dinners. Don't let them know there's a panic. Jed, I'll come with you. We'll try and catch him with the rowboat. Sarah, ring the coastguards, tell them what's happened.'

Mrs Fielding had heard the commotion and run down the stairs. She was now sobbing uncontrollably.

Peter patted her shoulder. 'Now, Mrs Fielding, everything will be all right. You stand by the phone and get ready to instruct the coastguards if they need directions. We need you here with hot drinks and a welcome hug when we bring Danny back.'

Her sobs subsided and she wiped her eyes. 'Of course,' she whispered. 'I'll be all right. Just bring him back!'

Jed was already out the door and Peter ran after him with Sarah. Davinia bustled away to the kitchen to calm a flustered Molly.

They stood on the rocks and, with sinking hearts, realised that the ebbing tide had already carried Cynthia a long way beyond the waves. Peter trained his binoculars on the boat and smiled grimly.

'Well, I can see him!' he said. 'He's on deck, hanging on to the side. As long as he doesn't try to get off the boat, he'll be OK.'

Jed was already dragging the rowboat into the waves and he and Peter grabbed the oars and put out to sea. The waves splashed over them and Sarah shivered. They were going to be very wet and cold when they returned. She held her mobile to her ear and dialled the coastguard again, updating the information she had already given them.

'They're on their way,' was the cheering message and she saw the lifeboat in the distance, as it shot away from the harbour in Tremaine.

'Thank goodness,' she muttered and ran back to Rainbow's End to tell them the news.

Using Peter's binoculars, she watched as the lifeboat approached Cynthia. Jed and Peter were still a distance away but both were pulling hard on the oars. The two boats neared the bobbing Cynthia and Sarah heaved a sigh of relief as she saw minute figures board the fishing boat. She waited tensely. As long as Danny had remained on board, there would be no problem.

The lifeboat arrived at the jetty first, a burly man carrying an excited Danny in his arms.

'I went fishing,' Danny announced, a big grin on his face. 'And I've been in a lifeboat!'

Unaware of the panic he had caused, Sarah managed a weak grin as she hugged him. 'Thank you so much,' she whispered to the rescuers. 'I must ring his mother and let her know he's safe.'

'I'd like to know how he managed to release the boat,' the man said sternly. 'It can't have been tied up very safely. But,' his face broke into a grin, 'he's a chirpy little chap and at least he's not come to any harm.'

'It's Jed's boat.' Sarah looked behind him to where Peter was tethering the rowboat. 'He's bringing it in now. I'll take Danny home, if that's all right and perhaps you'd like to come up to Rainbow's End for a drink?'

'Better get back, miss. But thanks anyway. If we need any more details for our report, we'll call you. In the meantime,' he turned and watched as Jed eased Cynthia into the jetty, 'I'll have a word with the boat's owner.'

Sarah put her arm round Danny and guided him up the path to Rainbow's End where his mother enfolded him in ecstatic hugs before scolding him. Not in the least daunted, he chattered excitedly about his adventure as she took him upstairs.

Sarah went into the kitchen to relay the details to Davinia and Molly as she gratefully accepted a steaming mug of chocolate.

'So, all's well that ends well,' Davinia smiled. 'Where are Peter and Jed?'

'They're having a word with the coastguards and then they'll be here. They're rather wet so I'm sure they'll appreciate a hot drink. How was the dinner?'

'Wonderful.' Molly was beaming. 'Everything was just perfect and they ate every scrap. No complaints tonight. They've all gone off in their cars and I gather they're leaving first thing in the morning. I've promised them an early breakfast of croissants and jam!' Molly sniffed. 'What's wrong with bacon and egg, I asked myself. Never mind, it'll mean less work.'

'And Alan?'

'He's gone with them. Not much to say for himself, that one. They were all clapping him on the back and saying what a good time they were having. Not that he looked pleased at all. Funny man!'

Jed and Peter arrived rather wet and bedraggled. Peter looked exhausted and Davinia fussed round him, insisting he went for a hot shower as soon as he had finished his drink.

'I've kept your dinner warm.' She shooed him out of the room. 'Go and get into something dry and then you can eat.' She followed him into the hall and Sarah turned to Jed.

'Trouble?' she asked. He shrugged.

'They weren't too happy about the fact that a five-year-old boy had undone my mooring rope and I still can't understand it myself. But he's a determined kid, and I haven't been down to Cynthia for a couple of days. The knots could have worked loose, loose enough for him to untangle anyway. I've promised to get a chain as well, just to be sure it doesn't happen again. Anyway, I think I'll turn in if you don't mind.'

'Will you have something to eat with us, Jed? Please?' Sarah longed to put her arms round him. She was so thankful that Danny was safe and her emotions were rather wobbly, but he turned away and shook his head.

'Thanks, but no. Goodnight everyone.' And, without a glance at Sarah, he left.

The sun woke her, catching her eyes through a chink in her curtains. She was surprised to see it was nearly seven. She switched on the kettle and opened the curtains to a glorious morning and her heart lifted. Refreshed from sleep, the world looked happier and she vowed she would make up her row with Jed at the earliest opportunity.

Besides which, she acknowledged to herself at last, the feelings she had for him would not go away. She wanted to get to know him better, feel the strength of his arms around her again, taste the saltiness of his kiss . . .

Shaking herself from her daydreams, she hummed to herself as she prepared for the day.

She wouldn't have been so happy if she'd been able to read Jed's thoughts as he prepared for the day. He had slept badly. The appearance of Marcia had devastated him. He had thought that period of his life well and truly closed.

He had woken up one morning and seen his future neatly planned, with no adventure left. The shock of realisation had panicked him and he hadn't dealt with the broken engagement at all well. He was still rather ashamed of the way he had run out on Marcia after their row. He had since written to her father apologising for his behaviour, which had eased his conscience a little, but the sight of his ex-fiancée on the doorstep at Rainbow's End had more than shaken his equilibrium.

He couldn't blame Lucy. She hadn't known the details of his traumatic break-up and no doubt Alan had manipulated her in the same manner as Marcia had manipulated him; but for Alan to bring her here! Jed was still reeling from the shock.

Clutching his precious freedom to his heart he was looking at his present position with a new perspective. Marcia had finally gone, that much was certain, but how did he feel about Sarah? There was no doubt in his mind that he was falling in love with her.

But, could he commit himself to a life fulfilling her dream? Would he get itchy feet again when Rainbow's End was up and running, and long for his freedom? He'd hardly had six months on the road yet, and here he was, contemplating curtailing the very thing he valued more than anything else.

He was scared. Love had sneaked up on him without his consent, much as his engagement to Marcia had sneaked up on him. Of course this was different. Sarah was in no way manipulating him towards an engagement. In fact, he thought to himself, Sarah had made it plain she wasn't interested in commitment at present.

So where was the problem? Neither wanted a romance, but neither had bargained for that little emotion called love!

Jed sighed and surveyed the orchard. He loved it here. But he needed time to think, time to clear the debris of the past from his mind, time to decide what it was he wanted from the future. And the last thing he wanted to do was to hurt Sarah. No, there was only one solution, and the thought of that weighed heavily on his heart.

Meanwhile, Sarah gaily went to say goodbye to Alan's group. They all seemed in high spirits despite the early hour and shook her hand warmly as they loaded the cars.

'Thanks, Sarah, we've had a great time.'

'We'll be back!' A promise Sarah wasn't sure she wanted them to keep.

Only Alan looked subdued as he came down the hall with his case.

'Goodbye Alan. I'm glad the conference was a success.'

Sarah saw the cars depart down the drive with a feeling of relief. Thank goodness that hurdle was over. Now, she must organise the cleaning of the rooms. Another family and the walkers were arriving this afternoon and the Fieldings had decided to stay an extra couple of days.

After lunch she set off for Tremaine with a light heart. She had some business to complete and then she wandered down to the quay. Boats bobbed in the sunshine and tourists clicked cameras at the picturesque scene. She saw Lucy sitting on the low stone wall and walked towards her.

'Hi, Lucy, everything sorted?'

Lucy turned and smiled. 'Thanks, Sarah. Almost I think. I was going to come up to Rainbow's End and thank you, but I was waiting for the final OK from Alan.'

'That's all right, Lucy. I thought Alan would solve the problem. What are you going to do now?'

'I thought I'd stay in Tremaine a while. It's a nice flat at Mrs Williams' and I've got my small job with Sebastian.' She blushed.

'Who's talking about me?' The voice behind them startled Sarah. Sebastian stood, a smile on his faced, gazing at Lucy fondly. 'Hello, Sarah.'

She studied him again, and she knew she had seen him before. 'I hear Lucy's staying on?' she smiled.

'Yes.'

'Sebastian wants to have an exhibition in London,' Lucy interrupted excitedly. 'I've a friend with an art gallery and we're going to see him next week.'

'I'm glad to hear it.' Sarah smiled at Sebastian who had been watching her. 'That's good news?'

He nodded. 'It'll be wonderful, if it happens. We'll see. Found your roots yet, Sarah?' He changed the subject abruptly and Sarah was startled.

She shook her head. 'I've had so little

time to explore yet,' she answered. 'Everyone seems to remember my father, but few people have actually given me any information about him.'

'He was born in Stoney Cottage.' Sebastian pointed to the stone cottage on the side of the harbour.

'He was? Did you know him?'

Sebastian shook his head. 'My parents did. That's his birthplace, Sarah.'

Sarah stared at the pretty cottage with a feeling of sadness. She wondered why her father had never returned and then, she thought, perhaps he hadn't wanted to see strangers living in his home.

'My grandparents?'

'They passed away, many years ago.'

Sarah nodded. That was what she'd been told. 'So,' she said softly. 'That's where my father spent his childhood. Who lives there now?'

'I must get back to the shop.' Sebastian looked at his watch. 'I hadn't realised it was so late.'

'I'll come with you.' Lucy followed him and Sarah sighed.

She must return to Rainbow's End too. Perhaps she'd ask Molly about Stoney Cottage. Perhaps whoever lived there now would let her look around. Her father's home; taking a last look she headed back to the car and her hotel.

When she arrived Molly called her into the kitchen.

'Problem Molly?'

'Well, sort of.' Molly was icing a cake.

'What sort of?' Sarah was getting fed up of problems. 'What's happened now?'

'I asked him to wait. Said as how you needed to speak to him, but he wouldn't take any notice of me.'

'Who, Molly?'

'Jed.' Molly said with finality. 'He's gone.'

'Gone?' Sarah echoed. 'What do you mean, gone?' Her heart plummeted.

'Just that, he's gone.'

'Where, into Tremaine?' Sarah was

grasping at straws and she knew it.

Molly shook her head and stood back to survey her artistic efforts on the cake. She cast a sideways glance at Sarah, her eyes anxious. 'He's driven off, with his caravan.'

Surely he wouldn't have left without saying goodbye? But then, she remembered his words in the kitchen, before the dinner drama. He had come to tell her he was leaving.

Sarah sat on one of the swings and gently let herself drift below the apple tree. The breeze brushed her hair and she surveyed Rainbow's End. All her dreams had materialised in this one beautiful spot. But suddenly, without Jed, her dreams seemed extremely sad and empty.

He was owed wages. Would he come back for them? It was a slender hope, but one that her mind hung on to. Perhaps wherever he decided to seek work next would ask for a reference and then at least she would have a contact address. And the boat Cynthia was still moored on her jetty. She wasn't going to give up hope that easily. Grimly, she stopped the swing and walked slowly across the empty orchard.

10

'What did Jed say, Molly?' Sarah was sitting forlornly in the kitchen, unable to take it in.

'He wouldn't say much. Said he'd called in to say goodbye — you know about it — and to tell you.'

'Did he say he was coming back?'

Molly shook her head. 'Said he needed some time to himself and would be in touch.'

Sarah had to be content with that. 'I suppose I'd better advertise for a replacement,' she said finally.

'I'd leave it a while. The youngsters are strong enough to help carry cases and there's nothing hurting at the moment. He'd finished all his work.'

'And the gardens?'

'My George will help out there, if you've a mind. He's a good gardener.'

'Thanks, Molly, that would be great.

I don't want the gardens to be neglected. They look so lovely.' She spoke wistfully.

'Oh, by the way,' Sarah remembered her meeting with Lucy, 'Sebastian tells me that my father was born in Stoney Cottage.'

'What else did Sebastian say?'

'Nothing much. We were interrupted.'

As they were now by a ring at the doorbell. Molly heaved a sigh of relief. 'That'll be the new guests.' Sarah took a deep breath and pasted a smile on her face. 'Ah well, business must go on.'

But it wasn't a guest that stood on the doorstep. It was a woman that looked vaguely familiar. 'Hello, Sarah,' Susan said quietly.

'Ah,' Sarah remembered, 'I met you in Tremaine Stores. Susan, isn't it? Come in.'

She held the door open and led the way into the lounge. 'Would you like coffee?'

'Thanks that would be lovely.'

Sarah went to the kitchen. 'I've got a visitor in the lounge, Molly. Could you get Jennifer to bring in coffee?'

'Guests?'

'No, Susan from the village.' Molly dropped a spoon and stared at Sarah.

'Susan?' she repeated. Sarah nodded.

'I'll bring the coffee.' Molly bustled to the kettle, her gestures agitated.

Puzzled Sarah returned to her visitor. 'Now, Susan, what can I do for you?'

Susan immediately jumped up from her chair and wandered to the window. 'I thought it was about time I visited,' she said and Sarah waited. 'It's about Roger, your father.'

'Yes?' Sarah spoke eagerly.

'Well,' Susan bit her lip, 'my name's Susan Morgan.' She waited for Sarah's reaction but Sarah stared at her blankly.

'Morgan,' Susan repeated.

'My father was a Morgan. We're related?' Sarah was startled. 'You mean I have relations here and nobody told me?'

'I thought it was time you knew, as

159

you're staying.' Susan sat down again and Molly entered. They exchanged looks.

'Well yes, I intend to stay.' Sarah smiled. 'Now tell me, what relation are you?'

'It's a long story.' Susan sighed. 'I'd best tell it from the beginning.'

'Carry on.' Sarah's heart was beating fast as she waited apprehensively.

'Well, Roger was born in Stoney Cottage. So was his brother.'

'His brother?'

Susan nodded. 'His brother, David. I lived in Tremaine too, my parents ran the Stores then, well, anyway, we all grew up together. They were different, those boys. Roger always wanted to get on, to get out in the world. He went off to college to study finances or some such thing.

'David loved the sea, like his father.' Susan's voice softened. 'He was never one for schooling, rather be out on the boats. When his dad and mum died he moved into Stoney Cottage, bought

Roger out you might say. Roger was settled by then, working in the city. He wasn't going to come home.' She took a sip of her drink and stared at Sarah.

'Go on,' Sarah said gently, realising, for some reason, the tale was difficult for Susan to tell.

'Well,' Susan took a deep breath, 'when we were young, it was your dad I walked out with. He was so full of life, so full of enthusiasm. Going to conquer the world, he was.' Susan's eyes were far away as she recounted the past.

'When he was at college, he'd come home, such a man of the world, so smart and he'd bring lovely presents. Anyway, we got engaged.'

'Oh!'

'But then he wanted to settle in London. I visited, but I could never have been happy there. Great big, dirty old place.' Susan shuddered. 'I tried really, but it was no good. I had to come home. Roger refused to come back with me. We had the most terrible row.'

Susan's eyes filled with tears and Sarah listened spellbound. 'Of course I was upset, but David was there, the sort of man I wanted to marry, he loved me and I came to love him too. He's such a kind, gentle man. Roger never answered my letters so, the upshot was, I married David.' She glanced quickly at Sarah. 'I've never regretted it mind. He's been a good husband and we've been happy.'

'Of course,' Sarah murmured.

'The tragic thing was though,' Susan continued, 'about a week after the wedding Roger came home. Said as how he couldn't live without me and that he'd set up a business in Tremaine if I'd marry him. Apparently he'd moved flats and didn't get my letters. Of course, by then, it was too late. David and I were wed. It was such a shock to Roger.'

'I'll bet.' Sarah was astonished by these revelations.

'Roger blamed David, said he'd taken advantage of me when I was vulnerable. All sorts of things were said that shouldn't have been. You know how it is, the closer the tie the worse the fallout.'

Sarah nodded, her thoughts flashing for a moment to Jed.

'David and Roger had the most tremendous fight, it almost came to blows and nothing I could say would stop them. Roger left, saying he never wanted to see David again. And he didn't!' Susan was tearful.

'I kept thinking Roger would come back, or David would write to him, but they were both as stubborn as one another. Time went on and we heard Roger had got married — a friend of mine had moved to London to get wed.' Susan smiled ironically.

'She lived not far from Roger and your mother and she kept me informed. David didn't want to know of course, so I kept the news to myself. I heard when you were born.' She smiled at Sarah. 'I did so want to heal the rift then, because I'd had a little boy, Sebastian. I desperately wanted him to know his cousin.'

Sebastian, her cousin, things were beginning to make sense. 'Did Sebastian come to Dad's funeral?' Sarah asked, light dawning.

Susan nodded. 'We were devastated when we heard Roger had died. Suddenly it was too late. David took it badly. He'd not long had a heart attack and the news hindered his recovery. But it was too late, we couldn't bring Roger back and we couldn't heal the rift. David's never got over it. I think he thought that one day . . .'

'So Sebastian was there, at the funeral,' Sarah recalled now. No wonder she had recognised him.

'David was too ill to travel and I stayed at home with him. Sebastian knew the family history and felt he should attend. He only went for the service and then came home. He saw you though. He wanted to make contact but felt it wasn't the right time.

'He intended to come and see you after the funeral. But somehow the years slipped by and then, before we knew it, you were here, on our doorstep.'

'And no-one told me.'

'Molly wanted to. She knew you'd find out sooner or later. But she felt it should come from us. She was right really. It's just taken me time to pluck up courage.' Susan smiled nervously at Sarah.

'So,' Sarah smiled back, digesting all the information, 'you are my Aunt Susan?' She laughed suddenly. 'I also have an uncle and cousin I didn't even know existed!'

The thought was amazing and she shook her head. Susan relaxed. She had been afraid of Sarah's reaction but now; perhaps the family rift could be healed, even if it was too late for Roger.

'Can I tell my mother? She's staying here at the moment.'

'Of course.' Susan wasn't sure how Davinia would react but the secret was out now.

'I wonder, would you like to bring

your mother for a cup of tea, maybe tomorrow? Then we can all get to know one another?'

'That sounds wonderful.' Sarah stood up and embraced her newly-acquired aunt. 'Thanks Susan for being honest. You've cleared up a lot of mysteries for me and I'm rather pleased to find I have a family after all. I just wish that Dad . . . '

Susan patted her on the shoulder. 'Never mind, my dear. Perhaps he'll be listening from where he is.'

Sarah liked to think so and after she'd seen Susan depart down the drive she ran to discuss the whole new situation with Molly, and to chide her for keeping the news of her family from her; although she understood the reasons.

Davinia was amazed by Sarah's news and not a little put out to hear about Susan. 'I knew he had had a childhood sweetheart,' she acknowledged. 'But I didn't know he'd been engaged, or about the family rift. He never actually said he hadn't got family, but as he never mentioned relations I assumed he was alone in the world. Well, I never.' She pondered on her husband's secret. 'Fancy that, and I thought I knew Roger so well!'

But the next day, as they sat in Stoney Cottage, both Davinia and Sarah made immediate friends with David and Susan. Sebastian called. Slightly apologetic for his part in the secrecy but Sarah hugged her cousin warmly and assured him they would soon be the best of friends.

The next few days passed peacefully with guests arriving on time, and no apparent problems.

Davinia was departing for London, Peter's leaflet had turned into a book and Davinia was going to sound out one or two publishers on his behalf. She came to say goodbye to Sarah.

'Thanks for all your help, Mum. We couldn't have managed without you.'

Davinia laughed. 'How could I not help, when the problem involved eight men? It was fun, Sarah.'

'Do you think you might get a publisher interested in Peter's book?'

'I think so,' Davinia said thoughtfully. 'Factual books are in demand at the moment. And I've one or two friends . . . I shall be knocking on a few doors, so we'll see. I must admit I'm rather impressed myself. The detail and photographs are excellent and he knows how to make facts interesting.'

'Well, I hope you're successful.'

'Peter might be joining me in London next week,' her mother said coyly and Sarah noticed a blush darken her cheeks. 'I thought I'd show him a few of my favourite places and he wants to go to the theatre.'

'That sounds marvellous. I'm sure you'll give him a good time. Just don't rush him off his feet, will you.'

'Oh, no, there'll be plenty of time for relaxation. And, now he's finished his book, I might be able to find out a bit more about him. I really like him you know, Sarah.' She looked at her daughter anxiously.

'I know, Mum,' Sarah replied quietly. 'He's a lovely gentleman.'

'Not like your father of course.' Sarah could hear the slight guilt in her mother's voice.

'No-one's like Dad,' Sarah agreed. 'But it's been several years, Mum. You're lonely. Peter's adorable and I'm sure Dad would have wanted you to be happy.'

Davinia's eyes filled with tears. 'I have grown terribly fond of Peter.'

'Then go for it, Mum.' Sarah kissed her mother. 'Have a safe journey and don't worry.'

She waved to her mother fondly and, with a sigh, returned to the daily routine of Rainbow's End. She was determined not to think of Jed, but at the bottom of her heart a small spark remained stubbornly hopeful of his return.

That hope was finally extinguished when she looked out on the jetty next day. Each morning the sight of Cynthia bobbing on the tide had been a promise of his eventual return. Today the boat had gone. Sometime in the early hours of dawn, Jed had managed to return and sail the fishing boat away. Her last tenuous link with him had disappeared.

She thought of him on the jetty, untying Cynthia and rocking gently away on the tide, the engine noise hidden by the sound of the breakers. When Jed had been so near, she had been sleeping. Tears poured down her face and she wiped her cheeks angrily.

Life settled into a peaceful routine. Only Sarah's heart remained unsettled, thoughts of Jed disturbing her frequently, however much she pushed them away.

And then, one glorious September day, when the heathers on the mountains sparkled in lilac and purple hues, and the wind was cool from the breakers that tossed over the empty jetty, she glanced out of the front window. There, parked on the drive was a caravan, a bright yellow caravan with blue daisies painted over the sides.

She rushed to the front door. From the familiar car, Jed unwound his large frame, the red T-shirt stretching tightly across his shoulders. How she'd missed his red T-shirts! Her eyes misted over as he approached her.

'I understand you're looking for a handyman, ma'am.' His face was deadpan. 'If it's not too late in the season, I should like to apply?'

He stood there, his expression wary and just for a moment Sarah hesitated. Then she flung herself into his arms. She felt his arms flex against her back.

'Oh Jed,' she sobbed into his T-shirt, all her defences crumbling in one emotional second. 'How I've missed you.'

'I've missed you too.' His voice was muffled into her hair. 'Oh, Sarah,' he held her away from him, 'I had to come back. I love you.'

They stood, clinging to one another,

their emotions too raw for words. Sarah buried her head in the familiar red T-shirt and felt the heat of his body through the dampness of her tears. He loved her. She wondered if she was dreaming; she had fantasised about such a moment so often, but she had never really believed . . .

But there was no fantasy in the crushing arms that almost suffocated her, no dream in his words. This was for real!

'I love you too, Jed.' She wiped the tears from her eyes and laughed. 'Now if you'd like to get Cynthia off my drive and back where she belongs, perhaps we can talk. There are a few things I need to say to you!'

'Yes, ma'am.' Chuckling delightedly, he curled himself back into the car and started the engine. Sarah raced along the track to the orchard, her heart full of joy. Jed was home!

Molly looked out of the window wondering at the commotion and gave a sigh of relief.

'That goodness for that!' she muttered and returned to peeling the potatoes, smiling.

THE END

We do hope that you have enjoyed reading this large print book.

Did you know that all of our titles are available for purchase?

We publish a wide range of high quality large print books including:
Romances, Mysteries, Classics
General Fiction
Non Fiction and Westerns

Special interest titles available in large print are:
The Little Oxford Dictionary
Music Book, Song Book
Hymn Book, Service Book

Also available from us courtesy of Oxford University Press:
Young Readers' Dictionary
(large print edition)
Young Readers' Thesaurus
(large print edition)

For further information or a free brochure, please contact us at:
Ulverscroft Large Print Books Ltd.,
The Green, Bradgate Road, Anstey,
Leicester, LE7 7FU, England.
Tel: (00 44) **0116 236 4325**
Fax: (00 44) **0116 234 0205**

Other titles in the
Linford Romance Library:

MOMENT OF DECISION

Mavis Thomas

Benita is a dedicated doctor, but when questions about her professional competence arise following a street accident, she starts afresh as general assistant at Beacon House, a Children's Clinic. However, this brings new problems when she is faced with her boyfriend's disapproval, the Clinic's domineering but charismatic Superintendent, and the two disruptive children she befriends . . . and then she becomes the victim of a blackmailer! There are many urgent decisions to make before Benita's future becomes clear.

TO TRUST A STRANGER

Anne Hewland

When Sara Dent's landlord relinquishes his business interests to his great-nephew Matt Harding, Sara fears that she will lose control of her struggling craft shop. And what — or who — is causing the strange noises in the empty rooms above? As she becomes reluctantly attracted to Matt, she discovers that her sleepy market town conceals sinister secrets. Sara must undergo emotional upheaval and life-threatening danger before her true enemies are revealed, and she learns who can be trusted — and loved.

SHADOWED LOVE

Janet Thomas

Following a break-up with her partner, Helen Matthews returns to Cornwall to set up a bed and breakfast business in her inherited cottage. There, she meets the arrogant Martin Somerville, who offers to buy her land. Helen refuses, but she faces many more setbacks before she can realise her dream . . . And is it possible that she was wrong about Martin? Could they ever look forward to a future together?

HOME NO MORE

Sheila Holroyd

Emma thought she would be a wealthy heiress when her father died. Instead she is shocked to find she faces the prospect of having to sell the home she loves. John Burroughs is willing to help the lonely girl with this painful task, but what about Jed Riley, the wheeler and dealer from Liverpool with an eye for antiques? Which man really cares about Emma and which one has other motives?